MW01386202

Nine Frames

**Featuring the winners of
The Cunningham Short Story
Competition
2019**

For George and Renee

"… human life, seen through human eyes, sometimes fortunate, sometimes unfortunate, neither perfect nor imperfect; it simply was, and is …"

Robert Hamilton Cunningham, from the short story "The Dance", part of the anthology *Life Dances* (2017) edited by Trevor Maynard

FOREWORD

The art of telling a tale was first illuminated to me by my grandfathers, RH Cunningham, for whom this anthology series is named, and GW Maynard, to whom I have dedicated this volume and enclosed the short story "George".

My two grandfathers, Grandad and Granpop, were chalk and cheese: the 5ft 5" clean shaven, cruise ship steward: and the 6ft 2" market trader with the Father Christmas beard. But there were similarities; they both fought in World War Two, sailor and paratrooper respectively. Later in life they were both taxi drivers; and finally their ability to spin a yarn encouraged and influenced me to turn my tall tales into stories, plays and poems.

For me, remembering my grandparents is a personal journey. It is also creating an oral history, revealing individuals who have lived, honouring them is honouring all those who have had lives, and given their lives; it is bringing them to the present, so every reader gets a glimpse of who we all are, where we come from, and maybe where we are going.

From the many entries for the 2019 competition eight stories have been selected which most reflect this year's theme: lyrical tales about the world, either personal, natural, or political, which takes the reader on a journey to events and places which they may not be familiar with. Each tale is an original work which, hopefully, presents to the reader a new perspective of their world. The first prize this year was won by Mike Friers for "The Race".

The next submission window for the Cunningham Short Story Competition 2020 will open in the January that year.

Trevor Maynard, August 2019

Copyright Notice

Nine Frames
Maynard, Trevor (Ed.)
Willowdown Books
ISBN-13: 9781073411511

Acknowledgements
Front cover design © 2019 Trevor Maynard. Back cover photographs © each individual writer. Thanks to JE Bird, my family, my grandfathers George and Bob, and my cats, Willow, Boston, Lily, and Georgie Boy.

Nine Frames

CONTENTS

Starlight

By Piet Pedersson

Mornings were a time for freshly squeezed orange juice and, come winter or summer, hot buttered muffins with strawberry jam. Midday and the early afternoons were for snoozing, laying on the beach, probably a swim, then a sleep by four, in a stone floored, shuttered room, back and front doors open to facilitate a cooling breeze. It was in just such a way that the hours of six in the morning to ten in the evening were filled by George Fenwick, son of Douglas and Flora, nephew to Mabel, and ardent student of the constellations of the night sky. Therefore, it was beyond his comprehension why anyone on earth, in their right mind, would think it was in any way a good idea to take him on a summer vacation to Lapland.

Aunt Mabel: five feet nine, elegant in her silk flapper dress patterned with oranges and lemons, matching headscarf, and no shoes. Outrageously, she never wore shoes. Shoes were how *Men* punished *Women*; especially in Japan. She would drive the brand new open topped, claret-red, 1926 Renault 40CV, in which they were to take their journey. If his parents were apprehensive at all, they did not show it, in fact, they seemed to be quite overjoyed at the prospect of sending their only son two thousand miles in a death trap with a woman clearly a few pearls short of a necklace. They now even kissed in public, like *Continentals*, and Aunt Mabel openly laughed, showing her gold tooth.

"The joys of the open road, eh Georgie?" Aunt Mabel held the steering wheel with one hand and a cigarette holder to her lips in the other. Amazingly she drew smoke and the embers burned. She reliably informed George the racing version of this vehicle could reach almost two hundred kilometers an hour. "Hand me that flask," she cheerfully shouted above the wind, the speedometer nudging the limit of its scale. Now she let her hand drape over the side of the door, her fingers twisting and playing with the onrushing air; seemingly to use two hands on the steering wheel was not the proper etiquette.

"Your mother thinks you're Nosferatu," she yelled. George looked blankly. "The Vampire?" It meant nothing to him. "Because you sleep all day and stay up all night, so I suggested taking you to a place where the sun doesn't set for nearly three months." He shrugged his shoulders. It was patently untrue he slept all day.

After observing the heavens and noting down the positions of the planets, he always had breakfast, only dozed in the afternoon, and never slept until four pm.

Nothing more was said until Lyon, when she uttered a word George had never heard any civilized adult say, let alone a woman. The cause of the outburst was another car which swerved and careered in front of them, hitting another car coming from the other direction, and causing the 40CV to pile into the two of them. It was a miracle no-one was hurt; in fact, it had been a miracle that three motor vehicles were together on the same piece of road at the same time at all. Literally the whole morning could go by without another motorized carriage coughing into view.

"Damn! Damn! Double damn, and blast the infernal machine!" An American, driver of the second vehicle, a Mercedes, intoned. More profanity ensued, perhaps this is what George's father had meant about getting an education. For not any particular reason that George could identify, Mabel was removing her head scarf and shaking her long red hair over her shoulders; it cascaded to the small of her back. She struck a pose; literally, hips thrust forward, a hand balanced on the uppermost, and a cigarette, unlit, in her cigarette holder. Jack McCrae, the American, leaned across and lit the cigarette. The driver of the third vehicle was apologizing profusely in French, but no-one seemed to be listening.

Three weeks later, Mabel drove George back into Sainte Maxime; it was one in the morning and a beautifully clear night. His parents were still up, carousing the evening beneath the stars, and taking it in turns to look through

George's telescope at the rings of Saturn. George, carrying a large box from the car, walked silently through the house and down the path towards the beach. Taking his bearings above, finding the pole star, and then the Seven Sisters, he began to unpack his impressive new telescope, infinitely better than the hollow tube and a mirror his parents were using, and almost costing as much as the Renault 40CV.

They'd never made it to Finland, but Mabel had sworn him to utter secrecy about that. They had bought a book and read all about it instead. Jack had paid for all the cars to be fixed, took George and Aunt Mabel to Paris where George's silence was bought by purchasing several boxes of handmade chocolates, visiting Versailles, and arranging a meeting with Count Aymar de la Baume Pluvinel at the *Grandes écoles SupOptique.*

The Count was an elegant man in his 'sixties with a white untrimmed moustache, who indulged George's broken French, but he himself made no attempt at English. He recounted his observation of the transit of Venus in 1882, and a story involving Louis XIII and his great grandfather, or his great-great … George followed MaCrae's lead and nodded sagely. Of course, the whole trip was on what Mabel referred to as the "QT".

For George, it was not the secret about not going to Finland that would be the most difficult to keep, nor even the fact that Aunt Mabel and Jack McCrae hadn't had separate rooms at the Hotel Nuit des Étoilés, it would be the fact that he had met this famous French Astronomer and telescope designer. Still, the prospect of a baby sister meant his parents were too preoccupied over the following nine months for conversation; however, George did now occasionally take a night off from his observations to waylay their fears of vampiric tendencies in him. Nosferatu it seemed was a really unpleasant kind of chap and George didn't want to grow up to be like him.

Your Table Is Ready

By Gregg Voss

The bot spoke through its unmoving, unemotional horizontal slit, red LED eyes trying to make contact with Mel's baby blues.

Mel wouldn't give it the satisfaction.

"I was created to serve, and programmed to assume the role of maître d'hotel at this specific restaurant," it said. "I will create efficiencies, which, as you can surely surmise, will result in cost savings. My return on investment, if used at a full-time equivalency, will be 17 months, nine days and 43 minutes, assuming a start time of this moment."

Glasses clinked nearby as Ray, the human bartender, prepared for Cinturon's 4 p.m. opening and the Saturday evening flood of Chicago's hip-and-trendy crowd. Mel sat across the bar high-top from the bipedal bot, with its black outer casing and white faux-human face. Kate, Cinturon's owner, sat between them, assuming the role of arbiter for this discussion, but looking as if she was prepared to become a sports referee, a certain severity lining her face.

The bot's words were delivered in a male British accent. Not cockney, but smooth and elegant, as if it had been assembled in Buckingham Palace and had once served the new King William. Like a butler – Jeeves, maybe. Of course, if Cinturon had been a Tex-Mex eatery, it would have been programmed likewise. Maybe it would have worn a cowboy hat, or even a sombrero, Mel thought. Wouldn't that be a hoot?

While he felt the bot's hot mechanical irises probing his face for a defensive reaction to the proceedings, Mel knew he couldn't indulge that part of his psyche. Is it possible this…this machine *wanted* the maître d' position? Desire conveyed emotion, and bots weren't supposed to be feeling, thinking entities. They were simply programmed to do a job, or so Mel had read in all the restaurant industry trade publications, of which he had been a fastidious reader over the course of his nearly 20 years at Cinturon, the last eight under Kate's ownership.

Mel had seen bots in action before, and the early ones seemed awkward, clunky even, which had led him to the conclusion that the technology would never do a better job than a dignified, experienced human. But this one was different. It was a late-model R.A.B.—formally, Restaurant Automated Bot—purpose-built for the maître d' role and, as it had stated, programmed for the specific vagaries of Cinturon.

"Well, we've heard from R.A.B.," Kate said, pronouncing it like "Rob," as if it were a real person, before turning her attention to Mel. He had decided for today's job interview—debate?—to wear his customary tux with tails and red sash, his uniform for years as Cinturon's maître d'. "What say you?"

That was The Question, and it was finally time to answer. Mel had agonized over his response for the last week since Kate had pulled him into her office after a particularly trying shift and said that she was considering automating the maître d' position for the very reasons the bot had noted – efficiencies, cost savings and swift ROI. Plus, R.A.B.s had become ubiquitous in Rush Street bars and restaurants, the latest in a long line of status symbols.

To *not* have an R.A.B. said something, carrying with it the implication that it just might be falling behind. Indeed, Kate was one of the last restaurateurs to consider doing away with humanity in that position, mostly due to loyalty to Mel.

But rising costs and peer pressure? That was becoming another matter, even for a savvy business owner like Kate.

Hence, Mel's great leap into the unknown.

"Why should I remain maître d'?" he said, leaning forward just a hair and tenting his hands on the high top, avoiding the bot's head, which was cocked in his direction. "The most important reason is this: I know my customers, in many cases personally, and I like to think they equate me with a quality dining experience."

Before Kate could say anything, the bot spoke.

"I, too, am capable of that, and much more efficiently," it said. "When a customer walks into Cinturon, I immediately compare his or her likeness with online citizen identification files, then instantaneously analyze their recent social media posts to determine what their likely menu and drink choices will be that evening. Hence, service is faster and the customer is both satisfied and pleased."

Almost as an afterthought, it added, "My base technology is the norm in 94 percent of restaurants in a 12-block radius of Cinturon. Customers have come to expect this mode of service. Put in simpler terms, placing me in this position simply meets a customer demand."

Well, there it was, Mel thought. Unassailable logic.

He couldn't read minds and didn't care for social media, with all its narcissistic bombast. He preferred to have dialog with people, face to face. There was a certain elegance in the exchange of words between people, the use of gestures to make a point, an easy smile when a customer's table was ready. The occasional hug from a long-timer, the bodily warmth reminding him that he was doing something worthwhile.

So he made his case.

"I don't think there are positions within a restaurant that should be automated," Mel began. "Certainly, you could teach a bot how to prepare a drink …"

The bartender, Ray, stopped wiping a glass with a white towel and gave Mel a hard stare.

" … but there is nuance to that task – there's what a recipe tells you is the right amount of vermouth for a martini, but what if your best customer likes an extra-dry martini?" he said. "It's the same with the maître d' position, and I would argue that it is moreso in many cases."

"I fail to see the correlation," came the smooth voice from across the table. "Preparing a valued customer's favorite drink is a learned activity."

"Maybe," Mel said, "but how many cycles will it take to get it right? Consistent mistakes will frustrate a customer. As I'm sure you're aware," and now he looked at Kate, "that frustrated customers tend to tell other customers and share their experiences on social media."

"As previously mentioned, I have the capability to monitor social media posts to determine a customer's feelings about Cinturon," the bot said. "Should a customer become…disenchanted…it's an easy matter of offering something in exchange for an unfortunate experience. Data from organizations such as the National Restaurant Association and mainstream media sources indicate that customers can be forgiving when it comes to a mistake, if the restaurant 'owns up' to it. While technology like R.A.B. is not infallible, it is much closer to that aspiration than humans.

"But again, I fail to see how your example relates to the position of maître d'hotel, which is the topic of our discussion."

That brief moment where Mel felt as if he had gotten a solid punch on a larger, quicker opponent faded quickly. Time for an example.

"Let's say a male customer comes in with an attractive woman that is not his wife," he said. "What would your response be?"

The bot considered this for a long moment before responding.

"The databases I am privy to accessing would immediately indicate that this hypothetical customer is not married to this woman, and I would make an internal assumption that the woman is a friend or colleague," it said.

"But what if they are holding hands? Or kissing, for that matter?" Mel said. "As a human, I have to have both discretion and empathy in my position to, how might I say this without being vulgar, 'keep it quiet.'"

Kate surrendered a crack of a smile. She knew customers like that.

"I am programmed with full emotional capabilities, including discretion, therefore nullifying your argument," the bot said. "But there is something more important Kate might consider."

Mel looked at Kate, and Kate looked at the R.A.B.

"Melvin made $53,346 last year, after taxes," it said, and Mel sat up in his chair. How could it possibly know that?

"He also was entitled to health and retirement benefits," it went on. "Compounded over an additional 10 years of service beginning today, that is more than a half-million dollars that would be eliminated, allowing for many improvements to be made to Cinturon, or introduce the possibility of a second location in an affluent Chicago suburb like Hinsdale or Northbrook."

Kate raised her left eye. This was making sense to her. More disturbing, it was also making sense to Mel.

Thus, he pivoted to his schooling days, as a philosophy major at Loyola University. Oh, those days were so long ago, and he had never imagined he would use those learnings and constructs to retain a service job. But it was worth a try.

"Nietzsche said human beings put values into things," he began, but was cut off.

"In order to preserve itself," the bot finished. "Nietzsche also spoke of the ubermensch, or the 'over man.' I am that being, one that will be more effective in a crucial position such as maître d'hotel."

Mel leaned forward again.

"You're an unthinking, unfeeling can full of computers and wiring," he nearly yelled, then calmed himself. "You can't possibly 'know' our customers intimately in order to serve them appropriately."

"I beg to differ. There is no argument you can make to place shade over the fact that I am better suited to this role than you, and not only from the efficiency and cost savings aspects."

The bot turned to Kate, as if in triumph, though it had no facial features.

There it was.

Checkmate, and Mel channeled Scarlett O'Hara.

Where shall I go? What shall I do?

The bot was suddenly Rhett Butler and silently filled in the rest.

"All right, all right," Kate said, as she climbed out of her chair in her pants suit and sensible flats. The succulent scent of prime rib and twice-baked potatoes began seeping into the bar from the restaurant floor.

"I've heard enough. Here's what we're going to do." She gestured to the podium up front, the place where Mel had stood proudly for nearly two decades.

"I've seen you for years, doing what you do," Kate said to Mel. "I want to see R.A.B." Once again, pronounced "Rob." As if she was on a first-name basis with a damn bot.

So it had come down to this. A performance-based evaluation. Arguments apparently no longer mattered.

The three walked to the podium and stood at attention, as a short, thirty-ish man entered Cinturon, wearing a blue blazer, khakis and what appeared to be handmade Italian shoes, a burnt sienna hue. It was John Wisniewski, who worked in the Cubs' front office and was known among the team, and everywhere else in the city, it seemed, as Little John.

Mel stepped forward to offer salutation, but Kate touched his arm.

"Wait," she said, letting the word hang in the air as if to make a point.

This was the bot's show.

"Ah, good evening, Mr. Wisniewski…or if you will indulge me, Little John?" the bot said in as warm of a voice as a bot could, which seemed to be as warm as Mel on a good day. "I have had a Heineken waiting for you in the bar area. Feel free to enjoy it there, and when you are ready, we have your usual table prepared.

"Now, that," Little John said as he strode past, "*that* is service." Then he added with a grin, "Hey Mel, I hope this guy isn't trying to take your job, because he's good. Damn good."

Anthropomorphism could be a hurtful thing.

And so it went. The Parker newlyweds from Evanston—a glass of Malbec for her, a dirty martini for him. Smiles all around. White Sox outfielder Jordan Owens and a striking model-esque blonde named Mackayla, celebrating their recent engagement—flutes of bubbly for both, along with a plate of calamari.

"Oh my God, it's like he knows what we're thinking!" Mackayla said as she and her baseball beau departed for the bar to join Little John and the Parkers.

The bot turned toward Mel and Kate in apparent triumph, as if to say, "I told you so."

Or perhaps better stated in bot language, "My logic cannot be denied."

Kate was smiling by this time and had her hands on her hips, which said to Mel, "What I expected. What can you do?"

Instead, she said, "Pretty impressive."

Customers began flooding the reception area, and the bot picked them off one by one. More pleased comments, and the occasional, "Hi Mel," in passing, of course.

That wouldn't be enough to save his job.

"I think I've seen what I needed to see," Kate said. "Mel, let's go to my office and talk."

Mel got the "N" of the word No out of his mouth, but then stopped as an older gentleman made his way to the podium. It was Mr. Shannon, recently separated, wearing an Irish pub cap and a brown corduroy jacket. Of course, Mel knew him as simply Edwin. A retired Chicago business giant, who had helped orchestrate the dissolution of Sears way back when, had been coming to Cinturon for years and years. Mel considered him a close friend. In fact, he had had a heart-to-heart with Edwin about a very sensitive topic less than a week prior.

"Good evening, Mr. Shannon," the bot said. "I have had your usual Brandy Manhattan prepared in the bar area."

Mr. Shannon furrowed his brow in apparent offense.

"I didn't come here to drink," he snapped.

"I apologize, but our data indicates…"

"I don't care what your data says. You're wrong," he replied.

Bots can't blush. They can only process data.

"Perhaps you would prefer a Guinness instead, considering you recently returned from Dublin?"

"What?" A vicious stare at Kate, who looked as if she was formulating a response, but was failing.

Mel stepped forward.

"Edwin, so good to see you. How's tricks?" he said with a warm smile, putting his arm around the older man's shoulders, then lowered his tone. "How are you doing with that thing we talked about last week?"

Mr. Shannon slowly shook his head. "I'm taking it day by day, and hour by hour sometimes," he said. "But I'm doing my best, thanks for asking. Can I get a table?"

"Of course," and Mel walked him to Table 29, far out of earshot from the podium.

When Mel returned, Kate was beckoning him with her right forefinger.

"What was that all about?" she said in a hushed tone.

"He quit drinking last week, in order to try to save his marriage of 31 years," Mel responded. "That's not something you post on a Facebook page. If he did Facebook, which he doesn't. He hates social media."

It was then that Mel realized the bot was staring at them. It said nothing, which was probably the logical response.

"Mel," Kate said. "Get back to work. R.A.B., come with me."

It still sounded like "Rob" to Mel.

Elan

By Kevin Michael Patrick

The evening glowed with a resonance that writers like; you know the kind of thing, mauves, magentas, scarlets, crimsons and hints of orange; fingers of light gliding, floating, reflecting, bouncing off the clouds and announcing sunset, it was romantic. Not only romantic, it was *perfect.*

We had just had a lovely meal at *Chez Michel* in Clapham, including a bottle of full-bodied, heavily tannined red, and finished it off with Michel's own Gallic version of Bramley Apple Pie and Custard (e.g. with Cassis and Courvoisier). She leant back and patted her stomach, then laughed into her napkin. We were both a bit full.

After the Gastronomy, we skipped into Central London on the Tube, and read the poetry printed up inside the scuttling carriage. From Wordology we moved to Astrology; I was Taurus, Claire was Virgo, then our rising signs, I was Virgo and she was Taurus. The night was light and airy, warmed by the sun now departed, but still creating silhouettes; Victoria Embankment was a picture postcard as we walked her shores. Our conversation was convoluted, but also fun, mixing Architecture and History, Rugby and the Horse Trials at Badminton We examined every statue standing, pondered what their subjects had been like in real life, then gauged the popularity of each by the number of small white gifts left by the local pigeon population.

When the full effect of food, wine and night air was at its height, we sat down in the gardens by the Houses of Parliament, listening to the lapping of the Thames and commenting on the reflection of the moon as it swept, *oh so slowly*, under Westminster Bridge. As I told you, it was romantic. I felt my timing, as they say in comedy, would be perfect.

"What!?" She screamed.

"I didn't think it was that unusual a request," I responded, the words in my sentence shrinking as I spoke.

"What!?" She burst into laughter. Not your normal, average, *oh I found something amusing kind of laughter,* but the full-blown, falling on the floor, can't speak because my sides are splitting cacklelation. *(So, cacklelation is not a real word, but you get the general idea.)*

"What!?" She screeched. Apoplexy approached her, joined her and was surpassed.

"It isn't that funny," I said with dignity.

"Marry you!?" The words left her lips like the reply to a Knock-Knock joke.

"It isn't that funny," I repeated with a vestige of dignity.

"Marry? You mean marriage?" She said. "With an aisle and vicar and all that kind of thing?" I felt this wasn't going at all well.

"Yes!" I gave Dignity one more chance to back me up, but it deserted me and ran off with the page boy who had previously told the Emperor about his new clothes. "Yes..." I said with the firmness of butter lacking refrigeration in the Sahara. The night was fresh with the odour of petunias and roses. The skyline etched with far-off illuminations from the drawbridge the American's thought they had bought and by the distant but attractive violet of the Lloyd's Building.

St. Paul's, apparently, is also lovely at night, if you're ever in the area, but not the Arc, the Shard, and the Gherkin. City Hall, the London Eye and Natural History Museum jostled too. It was a crowded architecture in my mind, an impossible reality that made perfect sense to me.

"I'm sorry," she said belatedly. Her eyes sparkled in the lunar luminosity ... *(OK, so lunar luminosity is a bit much, but when you're in love, you can't help it)* ... the moon was bright, and if ever there was a time, then this was the time. Even Valentino, in his great silent days *(and not so silent nights)* would have been jealous of the moment that had thus presented itself to me. On the other hand, Stalin put in his bid, and came up with a few purges to put me through. And so as the Westminster Chimes made it twelve and I added Buckingham Palace to the tour; Princes William and Harry on the balcony.

Claire said; "No. Of course not."

No on its own would have been crushing. *No. Of course not!* Was pulverising and then repulverising *(yes, yes, I am struggling, but I tell you, this was extremely bad!).* I couldn't cope with the rejection alone. The whole of London fell to dystopian destruction. I had to find someone to blame, and quick. Physicists came to mind. If, instead of sitting around pondering expanding universes and what a quark is made of, they had been figuring out how to manufacture a portable, pocket-sized machine for opening the earth beneath my feet and swallowing me up whole, I wouldn't be standing opposite the most beautiful woman in the world turning into an amorphous mess of magenta, red and mauve.

"You only asked me, for the first time, out last Friday lunchtime," she laughed and drank in the night air. I gulped some too but breathing seemed to have become something unnatural to me. I had become acutely aware of the particulate count in Central London. The wails of HG Well's Martian machines shattered my ears and shred the neurons in my brain. With the desperation of the Artilleryman from that seminal novel, I spoke in earnest.

"Four years ago, last Friday, we met." For a moment she was stumped, momentarily I rallied, victory flared in my nostrils…

"Oh, we met four years ago... " she smiled and looked away, in the tell-tale way of the flattered but not interested. Defeat deflated my nasal canals. *(You see by that expression how the romance is evaporating.)* "So why did you only ask me out last Friday?"

"Ah!" I said, or maybe I only thought "Ah". Whichever, I was only capable of weak exclamation by now, maybe not even that, I merely sighed. "Ah." Or maybe even whimpered, when you get down to that level of patheticness, who cares?

I looked into her eyes; green fireflies danced across a pale blue sky while a black rising iris heaved and shone with pleasure and compassion. You see, the whole point is, I was in love, and it was undeniably an incredible, sensuously exquisite, mind-crushingly terrific evening. London rebuilt, before the glass ogres, before the Eye, and there was a re-odouring of petunia and rose. I can do this; I can reshape the universe.

"Er …"

"Er... " I ventured, continuing to show off my monosyllabic dexterity. My mind turned over swear words in three different languages, eight different dialects and a host of as yet undiscovered lexicons, but even the ability to blaspheme profusely in eighty-three separate ways did not allow my brain to break through my own personal

Tower of Babel. "Mmm ... " I tried. The adding of a consonant to my vocabulary did not help.

When someone else is annoyed with you, you have all the powers of self-righteous indignation, hurt pride and common decency *(God Damn It!)* to fall back on. But when *you* are the one who *you* are annoyed at, all that is left for *you*, is self-pity. She had said *no.* She had said *NO. OF COURSE NOT.* What could I do now but crawl into my shell, curl into a ball and pretend to be a mollusc, waiting to be boiled and die screaming?

For a moment my mind wandered on this point, probably in search of one of those meaningful metaphors that novelists are so keen on. I visualized myself about the height of a pebble, and I was laying on a beach gazing up at a white-foaming wave which was just about to crash down on me. The water blazed with frothy white exuberance, promising everything, then fell limply, delivering nothing. Psychologists, well the bunch of them that deal with sex therapy, would say, men think of sex every six seconds. *Well, that really helps me, doesn't it?*

"Is that why you asked me out for this particular Friday?" Her voice echoed wetly in my dream.

"What!?" I continued with my monosyllabic show of intellect. There had, however been a development. I had abandoned vowel and consonant sounds in favour of an actual word.

"I suppose you are right," she leant back, her neck as... as Antony must have described that of Cleopatra; smooth as porcelain. *Romantic, eh?* She continued.

"Yeah, even forget my Mum's birthday sometimes." The corners of her mouth creased and her cheeks shone just that bit rosier. Her hair fell gently about her face, framing it like a soft-focus lens does in an old Hollywood movie. Everything was so romantic, she was so beautiful, it had been just the perfect moment...

"Er ... " I fell into linguistic relapse.

"Why didn't you ask me out four years ago? I would have said yes," she said simply, concerned for me now. She put her hand on my arm. Smugness, superiority and condescension dropped from her ruby lips like a ton of bricks from an award-winning sixties tower block now meeting its maker. Anger is a great leveller; it makes you coherent and suddenly you can see clearly.

"You were married to someone else at the time!" I spat, turning away for effect. Of course, saying she was married to *someone else* was a particularly stupid thing to say, considering I had just proposed to her.

"Gordon," she said, uttering my name as if it were a Chinese carving knife. "How many girls have you proposed to?"

The tidal Thames had retreated, revealing her rock and mud strewn flanks, seeking the comfort of the English Channel. But that rough, unpredictable expanse of water that had given us Her Majesty's National Xenophobic Government, was a cruel, gin-swilling old hag of a mother. She cuddled the infant river for a few brief hours before expelling her baby back into the veins of The Big Smoke, wherein she died twice a day of sewage and decay. *Unlike the kind of metaphors sought by creative types, the above is scatological in tone, reflecting my turgid rejection of Claire's shameful reaction of me.*

"Maria Gilbey, Carrie Frazer, Dawn Markham, Louise Collingdale," she calmly recited the litany of my previous failures. She had no conception of the grief she was causing. I could tell this by the way she cackled, like some pointy-hatted, broomstick-riding, wart-nosed ... God, she was beautiful! There is no way of getting away from that fact. It was impossible to be angry at her. To me, she is the subject of a thousand poems, a million melodies, and a fair amount of hyperbole. She is *(with apologies to Shakespeare)* the food that music be the love of.

"This is different," I said, surprising myself. Where was the sudden strength coming from? "I met you, I liked you, got to know you, became friends with you, *didn't sleep with you,* waited four years for you, and then asked you to marry me!"

There's a saying, always quit while you're ahead. I took the hint and stared into the night sky. The Milky Way sprinkled a path of platinum dust across the blue-black heavens. The moon was full and clear, I could even make out a few of the larger craters with the naked eye. As I said before, it was a romantic evening.

"It would be pretty stupid just to marry you," she said. Any hope that she had caught the last train to forgive-me-ville and left pity to crash down on the sofa for the night, evaporated. I felt like I was four years old again and my Big Sister had just ripped the head off my favourite teddy-bear. Curiously, the expression on Claire's face was the same one as my mother wore when I presented her with my decapitated best friend.

"I would have to be crazy," Claire continued. I stared into her eyes, I looked into her heart, and I wrestled with her soul - had this woman got no bloody sensitivity!

Only so much sand can be kicked in the weakling's face before even he stands up to his full height of two feet one inch and grabs his attacker where no man, or woman, should ever be grabbed in anger. I determined to tell her exactly how she was crucifying me, how she had made my life no longer worth living, and how she had made me into the victim of a cruel 1950's melodrama! Yes, I was going to tell her now. I wasn't going to beat around the bush. I wasn't going to prevaricate...

"Absolutely mad," her forked tongue whispered into my ear. My eyes were clogged up with hot tears by the wagon load, but they stayed in their duct, refusing to let those wagons roll down my cheeks; I had this great temptation to sniff, but finally, my saving grace, *Pride* came to the for. If she wasn't going to notice she had ripped my heart out, torn it into little pieces and stamped all over it, then I was going to pretend that it had never happened.

"It was a joke," I said and beamed. "Your face!" I poked her playfully, yet manfully in the arm. "Your face is a picture. Oh, come on, you didn't think I was serious, did you?" I stood up and stamped my feet on the floor as if getting rid of the cold on a Winter's morning. "It was just my little joke." She gazed at me; mouth open. "Come on, Claire. You didn't think I was actually serious? Marry you ... "I laughed and inched a couple of steps towards the escape gate, maybe I would be able to open it and survive with a modicum of dignity intact.

The chimes of Big Ben tolled - I don't know who for, but they tolled. The city was cold and hard around me; the London Eye unblinking, edifices of glass and steel once more callously offended, The moon was not silver, it was a rotten grey, like forgotten cheese, and the fluffy clouds that floated in front of it were the furry mould when you come back from your summer holidays.

The Milky Way was indistinguishable from the rest of the light polluted sky. The Thames Mud squelched with shopping trollies, and I was beginning to feel slightly sick from eating too much *French Traditional English Apple Pie.* Valentino would never come out on a night like this; you would be lucky to see old Stumpy himself, Walter Brennan, *and he probably wouldn't put his teeth in.* And she, Claire? She was not'in' special. Dirty green eyes, limp hair and big ears.

Hope was gone, and though I would never in the physical, mortal world, ever commit suicide, in my mind, I had electrocuted myself while falling off a cliff, having shot myself in the head with a shotgun and fallen on my sword. I could still smell the afterglow of natural gas from my oven, and taste the chalky unpleasantness of paracetamol and whiskey; yes, I had died in so, so many ways, and all in the two minutes since the words of my proposal had foolishly, tragically, left my lips.

"Maybe I am crazy," she said. I felt like a man who, two seconds after jumping of a multi-story car park, suddenly decides he wants to live after all.

What was she saying? My brain was not registering what my ears were hearing; or rather it had registered, but thought its auditory sense was deceiving it.

“Yes, I'll marry you," she replied.

Fireworks lit up the night sky, then I fainted, and we lived happily ever after.

THE RACE

By Mike Friers

The smell of exhaust fumes, the cold trickle of sweat snaking its way down his back, and, all around, the roar of the piston-pumping engines, intoxicated an already heady day in which Frank had moved from sixth on the grid to third, and was now coming up behind "Spy-Kid" Smith. Should he nudge the back bumper of Smith's 1982 Escort Estate with his front wing? A touch in the perfect place and his opponent's car would spin and career off into the unforgiving wire fence. Or should he dive down the inside, brake late, side-charge Smith and go for position?

Both strategies had downsides; Smith might not spin, or worse, his car might simply turn sideways, leaving both himself and his opponent dead in the water. More spectacularly, the spin might leave the car sideward; hitting a bump in the dirt track and then flipping onto its side, with Frank's joining it over and over with an airy roar as both vehicles, leaving the ground, rolled together like metal lovers thumping into a hard clay bed.

Which reminded him of Helen watching; thrilled at his gladiatorial battle, imagining him a Charlton Heston as he pushed the white horses forward, terrified and determined, life or death; well sort of. Perhaps she was unwrapping a Flake, letting the chocolate strands drop into her mouth and melt one by one; then again, probably not that either. More likely she was talking with his mother about the wedding, about floral arrangements for the church and table decorations, about party favours, and the guest list; one thing was for sure Ben Sheppard would certainly not be invited; what was she thinking? *His Helen.* Frank had no intention of inviting any of his old girlfriends he found on *Friends Reunited*, let alone his first love, why would she invite hers?

A shuddering jolt from behind, his neck whipping back so that his crash helmet tapped the roll cage; he was aware of the odd sensation caused by the car flying forward without him, until the force of the seat into his back propelled him forward. Frank was ahead, into second place, not through his own volition, but then again, who cared? Where was “Spy-Kid”? The answer was immediate; he came crashing into Frank’s back passenger door, while on the other side, Tom Collins (not his real name), slammed into him, gouging his drivers’ door. The effect was that as both drivers tried to spin him, so both pushed him against the other causing his car to hurtle forward, like a pip being squeezed from a lemon, catapulting him into the back of the leader.

He caught the old Rover ahead in just the right spot and its driver jinked left, then over compensated right and hit an almighty pothole. Instantly the driver’s front side tyre burst and the wheel dug into the dirt, tipping the vehicle onto its nose. It rolled alarmingly, head to tail, head to tail, in front of Frank, then off to his side, falling away from his vision. Frank told himself to keep looking ahead, keep going, don’t look back, don’t see what had happened, go forward, forward, faster, faster, his mind raced and his body caught up; he dragged his scraggy Renault into the lead.

One finger, held up by the starter, indicated his position as that of leader as he approached the line, and then three fingers, indicating the number of laps to go. Frank swore he could feel Helen waving her white scarf, and his mother, brother and sister, red faced in supportive yells. He was ahead, in the lead, for the first time, in any race – ever! Maybe his luck was changing; new job, new girlfriend (now fiancée), time healing the rift with his father? No, that was really just fantasy.

He thumped his left foot to the brake pedal and threw his car into the corner, making sure to force his right foot flat to the accelerator as well, then, lightening quick, to the clutch, shift the gear-stick, and pop out some more revs for added grip and a fast getaway. Time and heavy traffic had grooved and puckered the dirt track, creating a rough and ready Indianapolis Oval and the cars could bank at thirty, even forty miles an hour.

Frank quickly glanced across as he left the next corner, confirming that, due to their own personal battle, "Sky-Kid" and Tom Collins had fallen four or five car lengths behind. Before him there were four slower cars; one with a puncture fishtailing across the back straight; another petering out in a cloud of steam; the third knowing it was impossible to avoid both obstacles would have to choose which one to smack into, and therefore, the manner of his own demise. Frank would have to jink left, not too far, not into the fence, just enough to negotiate and lap the fourth car without either running into him, or having the guy become a spoiler (a back marker with no intention of winning, just the malicious intention of smashing the leader out).

Frank pulled it off successfully, but Smith and Collins did not. He could see them now across the track as he rounded the bend and joined the straight. He was away and clear, his next opponent half the track behind and as far as Frank could tell there were only six other cars still going. He let his foot lessen on the accelerator and his grip loosen on the steering wheel. Now he was leading, he had to control it, to maintain the position, there was no need to force the issue, no need to deliberately push when all that was needed was to finish. He had done the hard work. Now, he just had to avoid the metaphorical banana skin for another one and half laps.

This time he really did see Helen, waving her scarf as she said she would, and blowing him a kiss; it was beautiful, as if in slow motion, her face the centre of his vision, and everything around, hazy and out of focus. Then, near catastrophe, catching a rut, the back end of Frank's car slid out and clipped the fence, spinning him anti-clockwise, completely against the direction a car would normally spin on this track. His hand was thrown off the gear-stick as the battery, previously bolted tightly to the floor of the passenger well, shifted alarmingly but remained connected. Frank was sure he could hear the sharp intake of breath, the collective "oh" from the entire crowd, and more importantly, the abject disappointment from his family and betrothed.

Worse still, leaning through the windowless car from the passenger side, a marshal was shaking his head and shouting, and that marshal was his father.

"You're stuck on a tyre," he yelled, but Frank ignored him, finding reverse and roaring back, then forward, but the car was only stubbornly rocking. He realised with a pounding heart that the marshal wasn't actually his father, just an excruciating metaphor of gloating disappointment that resembled that cowardly deserter. Frank angrily crunched the gears, inventing profanities by the bus-load; there must be one that would work he cursed. The acrid smell of burning clutch was overpowering, while the noise from where the wheels only intermittently touched the ground served only to spur him on. He was absolutely not going to abandon this race now, this lead, this one and only time when everything in his life was going well, this one time when he was a success.

Then again, this was only a banger race, in a farmer's field in the middle of Essex, on the hottest day of the year so far. Emphasising this point, dust devils danced up a storm and suddenly there was no way to see through the muck and the grit. Suddenly through the suffocating brown haze, a stone flew through the air and hit the middle of Frank's visor. He was stunned for a moment, then petrified, convinced it must be a Stone Age arrowhead, sharp, able to split plastic and slice into his eye.

Another metallic thud meant another car had ricocheted off his boot, bumping him off his perch; he had finally escaped the demoralizing trap that had taken away his victory. Helen would be kind and consoling, she always was, she was good at sympathy, but Frank wouldn't be able to help but feel a failure again. His father had been a winner, over twenty-five trophies in three seasons, before he had abandoned the sport, along with his wife and kids. Frank however, had stayed involved. His brother stayed involved. Everyone was supportive. Their team-mates had become close friends. They, and his brother had found ways to overcome the difficulties, to keep Frank racing, determined to win, but in the end, it seems his father's favourite refrain had been proved correct, Frank had a snowballs chance in hell of ever winning.

Frank's dad had burnt his bridges, leaving Frank, even now, emotionally scarred by the fallout, he now couldn't hold onto a race he was leading by over half a lap. No-one could have caught him. The only enemy to Frank's success was himself, as ever, himself. Yes, Helen would be kind, but Frank didn't want that unavoidably cloying condescension. He wanted to be a winner.

Carefully he weaved around the pile up of cars on the back straight, avoided the Mondeo sitting on its roof at the top bend and as the dust cleared, saw the finishing line straight ahead. Two cars were wheel to wheel, side charging each other as they passed by the starter. Frank sighed; it looked like he would be third again, receiving a quarter-sized copy of the trophy the winner would parade in their lap of honour. It would join his other trophies for coming third and worse, in the case of his school swimming career, his commemorative medals for merely taking part; Frank finally had to accept the fact, he really was an *also-ran*.

He spotted Helen again, he knew she deserved better. She still waved her white silk scarf - surely it was ruined by the clouds of dust? His mother was still shouting, his brother and sister leaping up and down and then all four jumping into a group hug. Frank casually glanced to the side, at the chequered flag confirming his race was over; the pain of disappointment felt unbearable. He looked again, the starter was waving a single finger, as he passed - a single finger, his index finger, the gesture for indicating first, for winning, for being the winner. Frank had won the race!

He pulled up just past the line, unclipped his racing harness and heaved himself through the window and sat on the door frame, throwing off his helmet, and waving enthusiastically to the cheering crowd. His brother had leapt the safety fence and was racing down to help him, shouting "Way to go Frank!" A marshal hurried towards him as Frank tossed his walking stick out the window and onto the track. Frank lowered himself out of his car as elegantly as the situation would allow and grabbed the stick, expertly levering himself up straight, cautiously assisted by his excited brother. Helen held the scarf close to her face, staunching tears of pride, and mouthing the words; “You’ve always been my winner. I love you.”

The other contenders had been almost a lap behind. In the end, he was so far ahead; even being stuck, for what seemed like forever, was not enough to stop him. Everyone that mattered to him were around him now, they’d kept telling him he was a winner irrespective of the race, now he literally was, and had the trophy to prove it; full size. Finally, he had proved his father wrong. He should never have left, or written his son off, after the accident. Defiantly, Frank raised his walking stick and his trophy high into the air and kissed his wife to be; this was living.

Thumbs Up

By Teri Bran

Fortunately he had found the top of his thumb before the dog identified it as a tasty morsel, though it was close, Spencer was a bloodhound - well, in his mind - his body was that of a cockerspaniel/alsation/pug/collie mix, though what combination of parentage and how far back you would have to go before recognizing a full breed was impossible to know. There was surprisingly little blood, and apart from some slightly torn skin at the outer edge, the amputation was clean. Quickly he wrapped the excommunicated digit in a clean piece of rag, then, with that panic over, his mind decided to let him in on the full reality of the pain and shock. Paul fainted.

The nurse leant over him in an awkwardly fitting blue tunic whose straight lines did not fit her natural curves. She winked at Paul and his hand fell to the side, expecting cool white linen, but instead finding damp grass. He had not been taken to hospital, he was still in his back garden, and the nurse was his neighbour, Helen, who had a lazy eye, and was also a Major in the Salvation Army.

"Looks a nasty cut you've got yourself there," said Michael, Helen's husband, and a Colonel for God. Both he and his wife had been in their own garden practicing how to approach people with copies of the War Cry; Michael was naturally very shy and prone to ridicule by the local youth. It had led to agoraphobia, but the Lord had helped him through, and now Helen helped him do the rest. Spencer's tongue lolled out of the side of his mouth, as it was prone to do, and he panted heavily; he appeared to be smiling.

"My thumb! My thumb!" Paul was gripped by panic; the dog looked far too happy, the Salvation Army looked unconcerned, and he felt himself floating again, drifting out of consciousness; there were more people now, and all of them with haloes; strange, fuzzy, rainbow coloured haloes.

"Is he alright?" A sweet female voice asked. Paul wanted to say that he was alright, that he was perfectly capable of sitting up, of going to his car, of driving the owner of those exquisite tones to a country pub, of buying a bottle of Australian Shiraz – the one with the deep bloody hue...

The nurse leant over him, again, in an awkward fitting tunic, but this time with no natural curves to do combat with.

"I'm Paul," the nurse, in fact the ward sister, introduced himself. "Oh," he giggled. "And so are you, I see!" He may also have winked, or it may have been Paul's generally understated but, in this situation, rather blatant homophobia. He was on a small ward with three others, and two empty beds. Immediately Paul wondered if they had left, as John Wayne would have said, 'with their boots on'. The others, all women, all grey haired, all bespectacled, all reading glossy chatty magazines, did not return his need for reassurance. Paul looked slowly to his left, at his upper arm, his elbow, his forearm, his wrist, his hand, and finally, his fingers, but there was nothing to see, except bandages; his hand was in fact like a boxing glove of muslin, gauze, and webbing.

Paul was immediately transported onto a school stage, the show in imminent danger of being closed should the dominant curtains deem it not up to scratch, or indeed, in their infinite drapery wisdom, that a particular performer wasn't up to scratch. Paul's rendition of an eccentric Captain Hook swaggered in a way prescient to Johnny Depp's pirate, but for now, he just looked drunken, and as though he had forgotten his words. Cold sweat had trickled down his spine and puddled at the base, ready, when the liquid level rose, to breech the damn of his elasticised Marks and Spencer's micro fibre trunks and seep embarrassingly into his trousers. What was his next line? What was his next line? Tick, tock, tick tock, tick tock! Tick...

The alarm blasted and woke him instantly, but there was no clock, only his mobile phone, dancing on the bedside cabinet to the tune of Axel F – the version without the frog. Slowly he gazed at his paw, for it resembled the fur of a bear's paw rather than the shine of a boxing glove, and he wondered what was underneath it all. He also wondered what had happened to the carving he had been doing, and whether or not that last finishing touch that he'd been determined to get, had ended in the decapitation of his figurine, as well as that of his left thumb. Once again he saw Spencer, eyes sad and innocent like a spaniel, tail bent over backwards like pug, his long fur matted, like a sheepdog working in a muddy field, and his tongue bouncing around his mouth, slobbering and swallowing a piece of human flesh that was once his. Paul made a mental note – take the dog to the vet

"You've a visitor," a woman's voice, another nurse - another sister, informed him as she took his pulse and measured it by the watch pinned to her dress. "She wanted you to know she was here, and you're not to fall asleep as she's only parking the car," the sister was from one of those soft lilting southern states of Eire and the timbre of her pitch and tone, were indeed, proving a lullaby. Suddenly, at the back of his mind, there appeared an electrical signal, received from a nerve; a small, spirally nerve which effectively brought a message of exquisite pain from his hand, seemingly from the back of his hand, and it was then that Paul instinctively knew, the infection had spread – the bandage was masking gangrene; it would only be a matter of time before everyone would be able to smell the damage.

Instantly Paul thought of Wilfred Owen, and the First World War, with his cry of *Gas, Boys, Gas!* He thought of the injuries, the amputees, and of course, the long and slow painful deaths, hung over the wire in No Man's Land, twitching in premature rigor mortis, catching more and more stray bullets…

"Cheer up grumpy!" Monica, the sweet voice from earlier, and daughter of the God's Army Couple; he pondered what that made her. "Look what I've brought you." She seemed to teeter on tip toe, like an excited child as she brought an object from behind her back and placed it gently on the bedside cabinet; her head. Not her actual head, of course, but the likeness in wood Paul had been carving for months. He shrunk into his pillows, his secret discovered, and by the subject of his affection too; and he had indeed, chopped off her head. For a moment he visualized the woman standing behind Monica holding an axe, she even resembled Lewis Carol's famous Queen mouthing her famous refrain, but actually it was only Helen.

"And yes, I would like to go out with you," Monica held his good hand, but Paul shied away, trying to hide his bad hand, his injured hand, his disabled limb. "You only had to ask." She gave him a peck on the cheek, and her mother seemed to approve, obviously such sympathetic gestures were within the remit of the Good Book. "But now I've got to move the car again, only I couldn't find a space, and I had to leave Dad in the drivers' seat and in truth, he never learned to drive, neither of my parents did."

Paul suddenly felt he had something intelligent to say. "So, The Salvation Army are like the Amish?"

“Amish?” Monica looked at him as if he were mad; Paul clearly blushed, clearly he had demonstrated his lack of knowledge, and even prejudice?

“Oh, because they don’t drive, oh no, they just never got around to it.” Monica smiled pleasantly. Paul liked the sound of her voice wondering how so many words could come out in so short a time; her smile melted him.

“We never did get around to it,” Helen nodded as her daughter disappeared out of the door. She looked kindly down at him, and Paul felt humbled and grateful for the affection she showed for her fellow human beings. Paul was developing a real thumper of a headache now; ‘referred pain’ he’d been told, which could be eased by simple pain killers. Paul had palmed the last two Paul, the male sister, had given him, in some futile and pathetic attempt to prove his masculinity. Real men can stand pain.

“Nurse!” He cried. Paul returned, paracetamol at the ready as he poured the patient Paul a glass of water. “You’ll be taking them this time, then.” He grinned knowingly and winked.

“Paul! How are the wife and kids?” Major Helen asked. Obviously the pain was too much and Paul was falling into a delirium again, he had no wife and kids as she well knew, they had been neighbours for three years.

“Peter’s had mumps and Jenny knocked her two font teeth out when she ran into a post,” Sister Paul informed her, one hand on his hip, the other in front of his stomach. “Deena’s my angel, as always.” Three men and a woman, all in white coats arrived at that moment, and stood, hovering, waiting, and silent.

"Well, I must be going," Helen stood and with a cheeky grin, took a grape from the bunch on the bedside table. Paul turned his face away from the grinning world, away from the carved head, the grapes, and the cards. The cards? He had not noticed them before. He turned back.

"Paul, this is Mr Stanton," Paul introduced the oldest looking of the group. "He's the one that sewed your thumb back on."

"And a fine piece of work it was too," Mr Stanton stepped forward, the others remained behind, like hummingbirds, it occurred to Paul, for no reason he could justify in his mind – sewed his thumb back on? Paul sat bolt upright, so the dog had not been happy because of enjoying a snack between meals. "Shame we could only get it on backwards," the surgeon added, but his comments were guided back to his crowd, his audience, probably students; Paul understood that doctors toured their patients with hordes of clamouring medical undergraduates. Well, they had to learn somehow, he supposed.

"Backwards?" Paul suddenly realised what had been said. Backwards! Paul thought the whole point of humanity coming to rule the earth was because of their opposable thumbs and their ability to use tools. How would he now get on, having been surgically de-evolved to an ape?

"Just my little joke," Mr Stanton patted Paul on the shoulder and he felt reassured

"No gangrene, then?" Paul asked innocently. The surgeon swept his entourage off to the next bed, apparently only amused by his own jokes.

"Back again!" Monica seemed to appear from behind the flowers she was carrying. "Found a spot." She said and sat down, then stood up. "Oh, I bought these for you." Paul looked at the selection of daisies, wild grasses and heather. "Well not bought, chose – "she said and looked up at him from below long expectant eyelashes.

Paul no longer felt pain from his hand; either the pills had kicked in, or he was high on the knowledge that he wasn't maimed for life, he had survived! It could have also been that he had realised this was only a minor injury and he'd spent the day blowing everything way out of proportion, or maybe it was Monica's smile, her slightly parted lips now revealing the perfect white of her teeth, and forming the tiny creases at the corners of her mouth that he had captured so beautifully in his carving of her.

He picked up the head with his hand and rolled it around and laughed.

"Don't do that you'll make me dizzy," Monica told him and put her hand on his to stop the wood rolling. The touch was light, but warm, and he leant forward and she moved slightly too, just enough for their lips to briefly touch, then pull apart. Both looked self-consciously away. Three years he had lived next door to Monica, and three years he had fancied her; three months he had spent carving her likeness, thinking maybe, one day, if she accidentally discovered his work, she would know, and they would begin seeing each other. Perhaps his unconsciousness knew this and helped him out with a slight chisel accident.

Paul gently held Monica's hand and asked her to go to the cinema next Thursday; she said yes. He also decided to inform his consciousness to be less dramatic, and while he was at it, for himself to start imagining the positive, instead of the negative. Finally, he was going to have to apologise to his dog for all the bad thoughts he had been having regarding a future visit to the vet; animals have a sixth sense about such things, and Spencer would not be happy with anything less than extra fuss, extra walks and an extra jumbo sized bone.

Misanthropes

By Dean Gessie

Sally stared into the barrel. Through her own reflection, she saw small, beady eyes and big ugly snouts: dozens of small eyes, big snouts and movement that was pulsating and elegant. She did not start when she felt Jon's breath in her ear. His cologne was a blend of clean and dirty notes. That, and what he said, were equally ambiguous. She thought she heard the word, *berm*. If so, why had she blushed? She turned the word over in her head, producing rhyming couplets. The word, *discern*, all by itself, made no sense.

Sally continued to stare into one of the barrels while Jon talked. "These little guys are transparent. They've got eyes like peppercorns. These ones are adolescents or *elvers*. And I've got adults, too. The young ones swim here on the Gulf Stream. They go from flat to cylindrical. Anyway, they enter river mouths and penetrate upstream. Some penetrate overland. They're tough buggers. They used to be called *sticks*. They were good as money, once. Folk would take sticks for rent."

Sally looked through loose, grey bangs fluttering in the wind. "Why are you doing this?"

"The population's in decline," he said. "Who knows why? Parasites in their swim bladders. Pesticides. Weirs. Locks. Sluices. Anything hydraulic makes sushi of the best swimmers. My group has released fresh stocks in Blagdon Lake, North Somerset, Shropshire and Wales. We've got volunteers on four sites here on the Lymn. The goal is to boost numbers and -"

"*No*," she said. "Why are *you* doing this?"

"Oh, I've always loved eels with a passion. Decades ago, they moved like submarines along the banks of the Thames. After school, I'd scrunch me bum in the mud and spread a blanket –. Well, my heart still pounds when I see their shimmering bodies. Of course, a lot of fishermen don't like them at all. A hungry eel will swallow the bait right down its throat and constrict into a big slimy ball. Say, do you want to -?"

"What?"

"*Touch* one? Go ahead. Just stick your hand in and pull it out." Jon said the bite of an eel was no worse than the wound of coarse sandpaper.

Sally was still contemplating *fresh stocks*. She said she was all for reproduction, all plants and animals, everything. "You and I have that in common. I'm a conservationist, too. My *group*" she said, "is helping restore wetlands." She pointed in the direction of pink light on the horizon. "We've replaced oilseed rape with reed beds. And when the season and the wind are right, you can hear Natterjack toads and -"

Jon wasn't listening. He studied Sally's firm grip on the eel, how her thumb rubbed the velvety skin beneath its gills, how she seemed to inhale the eel scent. She had reached into the barrel containing mature males. Instinctively, the eel coiled around her wrist, like a snake cuff.

"Except for humans, of course. Humans can all die, as far as I'm concerned."

Jon's tone expressed surprise, but not censure, "What do you mean by that? You want all of us to kick the bucket?"

Sally returned the eel to the barrel and explained the Voluntary Human Extinction Movement. "We believe in zero population growth. Humans have already done enough damage. We want to return the earth to nature. For most, it's an extreme position. For us, it's a question of principle. I, personally, choose celibacy. My vagina is closed for business. Nobody," she said, "will be *boosting numbers* with this old slag."

Jon wanted to say that feeding time for eels was after dark, that they'll eat anything that drops to the bottom. But he was uncertain of his focus and timing. Instead, he pulled out, like a camera on a dolly, "When they find somewhere they're happy, they feed and swell and darken. Years later, some develop male sex organs. Years more, some develop female sex organs. The ladies won't be rushed into sexual maturity. Anyways, some live undisturbed in forgotten pools for decades."

"And you know all this because?"

"Surprise! I was a biology teacher." And he looked at her as a teacher might, with optimism and reflexive judgement. "Okay, so what did we learn today?"

"The young ones ride ocean current. They move from flat to cylindrical. They penetrate upstream. They penetrate overland. They used to be called *sticks*. Cylindrical sticks penetrate forgotten pools. They're all *tough buggers*. " Sally mimicked rote learning, but it didn't feel anything at all like that. "You see?" she said, breathless. "You really can teach an old girl new tricks!" Jon said he was absolutely sure of it.

*

Three weeks later, at the Revesby County Fair, she happened upon jellied eels at a pop-up shop for pie and mash. The vendor explained, “They’re shucked and boiled in water and vinegar. I add parsley, cayenne, nutmeg and other *magic* ingredients. Always good for what ails you.” He elevated chopped roundlets and lemon wedges on a paper plate. “Care to tuck in, luv?”

“God, no,” said Sally. She recoiled while shaking her head. She remembered the mucus and tumescence of the eel in her hand, the cut of its gill, the eyes and the swollen urgent movement.

“I would have picked you to swallow.”

“Jesus,” said Sally, “I was just thinking about you!”

Jon smiled and whispered, “I’m not alone.”

Whatever regret she felt became relief and then dismay.

“These are my kids. All eight of them.”

She looked at Jon’s brood. They were like eels in a barrel. Their movement was quick and their numbers shifted. The oldest boy, the only one stationary, said, “Are you the one that’s sworn off shagging?” He wanted a picture for his Facebook page.

Jon stepped between the two of them. He admitted explaining to his kids the politics of Sally’s zero population group. She did not listen. She suddenly had a better idea of that word she hadn’t quite heard. It wasn’t *berm*, but one of the others - *germ* or *squirm* or *sperm*. “I don’t mind,” she said. “I’m quite open about what I believe, what I do or don’t do.” She added, “And where’s their mother?”

Jon turned to his kids and said the terrier race was about to start. Elsewhere, there was falconry, horse tricks and a petting zoo. “Get off with you,” he said.

Afterward, he answered Sally’s question. “I talk about everything with my kids because their mother is dead.”

Sally thought better of castigating Jon for overpopulating the earth. She had intended to compare his breeding with the new avocet population in the wetland adjacent Gibraltar Point. And then she thought better, again. *One* gone and *eight* to replace her?

“Bloody hell!” said Jon. “What’s the difference? Zero or eight or five million. Yuh come at it from one end or the other and it’s all suicide, ain’t it?” And then he changed the subject. “C’mon. I’m going to take you to the movies.”

The cinema was a canvas tent in a cow pasture.

“Here, I’ll pay your ticket.” He added with a smile, “Maybe you’ll take a *stick* for rent?” There it was again, like his cologne, dirty and clean notes.

They found seats under the big top, folding plastic in air that was dank and dark. Few others attended. Sally thought of the petting zoo and terriers and falcons and horses. Jon explained that the films were archival, black and white footage from the libraries of the National Audubon Society. “I used to show these films to my students. Even then, they were old. The monochrome makes you believe there are only two time periods, nature and after nature.” Jon settled and added, “I guess that’s why most people dream in black and white.”

This particular clip jumped and skipped. It was a montage of magnificent swimming whales intercut with those who were harpooned and hacked to pieces with knives. Sally thought the *monochrome* enhanced the violence. And there was certainly no clear advantage to dreaming in black and white. Anyway, the sound of some sort of zipper distracted her from her anguish. And then Sally heard the protracted creak of Jon's chair, followed by a reedy whisper and a chuckle, "Touch one? Go ahead. Just stick your hand in and pull it out."

Sally remembered the script, that part about a hungry eel constricting into a big slimy ball around a hook in its throat.

*

Three weeks later, she saw him again at Croft Marsh. She now kept him on her species list, alongside oystercatchers, lapwings, Brent geese and golden plovers. There were no ticks for a number of elusive creatures, but Jon's many appearances were no less desired. He had clearly found *somewhere happy* or *a forgotten pool*. For her, it was different. Nonetheless, she did not choose to recognize him right away. She made him wait for hours. It wasn't until a water vole swam a path to his location that she relented.

"Are you a *twitcher*, Jon?"

"What's that?"

"A seeker of rare birds."

"Do you consider yourself a rare bird?"

"I do."

"Then, yes, I guess I'm a twitcher."

"And do you keep a life list?"

"Is that anything like a bucket list?"

"Somewhat. Do you find your rare bird, check a box, and then move on to the next?"

"I'm an eel man, Sally. I don't move on until it's time to die."

"That's comforting."

They walked all morning. At times, Sally passed her binoculars to Jon. He looked where she looked. Other times, he listened when she described the size and shape of birds, their colour, behaviour and song. She told him about a *hundred-year event* back when she was a *young chick* and how she made the trip to Larkfield to see a golden-winged warbler. "It probably came here all the way from Wisconsin. Can you imagine the beating of its heart? I felt more affinity for that animal than I ever have for the whole human race."

And she had him touch the water plants, too, those with leaves and stems and others that came without. He pressed his nose against plucked samples and inhaled greedily. And she described the seasons of cowslips and sea spurrey and brackish water crowfoot. And she saved her eye contact for that one time only, when she looked at him through her binoculars, surveyed the impression of depth, and said, "Human beings are *shit.*"

Immediately, Jon made winnowing eels of his arms and the pupils of his eyes, through objective lenses, became dark peppercorns. He didn't say anything, but Sally knew what he wanted.

She laid her camouflage hat in the sedge grass and decoupled her fanny pack and binocular harness. "Are you a tough bugger, Jon?"

He said, "The world is a big top. You swim or you get hacked to pieces." She didn't know if he was referring to whales or eels or something else.

After three months, Sally developed a kind of magnetic map. She no longer had any sightings, but she knew when he was there. One friend credited her with *intuition.* Another said she was a *horny cow.* Sally didn't know what to think, if the moon, the ocean or her own biological clock were clues in the ether. She *did* know that Jon was feeding, swelling and getting darker. And she knew that Jon knew her routines, that he didn't so much *arrive* as *wait.*

The mill at the edge of town was built of stone. Its cap was the shape of an onion bulb and made to move. In profile, the rear fantail, tower and sails produced a pied avocet. Sally had walked by the mill dozens of times, always counting the sail-cross of eight blades, but she was incurious or prudent enough not to enter. This time, however, she pushed the door - stiff and reluctant against the warped jamb - and reasoned her own interest as phototaxis, *like a bloody moth to flame*.

The question of how she knew of Jon's whereabouts was immediately laid to rest. It wasn't so much electromagnetism or intuition or moon tide, but *eel smell*. The dark, dank interior of the mill left her two things: olfaction and a fishy vaginal odour. Jon must have guessed right that day or dodged in and out of hiding over three months. Either seemed perfectly plausible to Sally.

The interior of the mill was tenebrous, but she could make out the largest parts of ancient machinery: a wooden upright shaft with a great spur wheel. Beyond the shaft and the wheel, only the stairwell made sense. She struggled to discern where she was going, letting her fingers ride the masonry. On the top floor, she couldn't see the blocked exit to the ground or the single blocked window. For some reason, she was sweating profusely and wet to the bone. She set down her camouflage hat and unclasped her fanny back and binocular harness. She sat and waited.

By the time her eyes adjusted to the absence of light, Jon had already started his lesson: "One dark night, usually after rain and with the moon covered, the females get the call. They've already turned mottled green-black on top and silver underneath. The anus constricts to reduce water loss and the fins and eyes grow larger. They head downstream on the flood and swim three thousand miles. Eventually, they all release five million germs into the primordial soup. After which, each and every one of those old slags dies of exhaustion. The good fight," said Jon, "is the only fight in town."

The monochrome setting and the perfunctory narration produced anguish for Sally, the feeling that she was watching an old nature film or her own dream, anticipating competing imagery of beauty and brutality. But these dissipated quickly when Jon fell upon her with something like poetry, "My heart still pounds when I see your shimmering body." And then his fingers became serpent cuffs coiled around the small bones in her wrists. And his last words anticipated her own stressed syllables.

"Easy does it, Sally. I'm not here to save you. I'm here to fuck you."

Of course, Sally already knew he was a bottom feeder, one with the whole lot. That's why she had come and why she said, "No, Jon. *Fuck you*."

White Flags

By R.D. Girvan

The Crosstown bus swerved around a crater and struggled back into its own lane. Eyes fastened to his brochure, Jack remained standing, a gas mask slung over his arm. The bus clipped the edge of a blast hole, jarring the commuters. He reached up to steady himself, his wedding ring clinking on the aluminium bar overhead.

Jack's grandfather would have said, "What season follows Winter in Edmonton? Construction." Not a lot of construction crews out this Spring, though; most people still standing were on Clean-Up details. Or had joined Removal teams.

The bus strained up a hill. Someone pulled the bell cord and the driver called out the next stop, "176th and Yellowhead Highway!" Jack scrunched down to see out the window. From this height he could see the precision, the efficiency of the Enemy's bombs. Behind a moat of tangled, twisted railway iron, the City's main railway depot – a carefully engineered, controlled chaos of lights and wires and switches and signals - lay, safe and untouched.

The Enemy strikes had pulverized the lines leading in and the tracks leading out. Jack had noticed, though no one else seemed to: they only destroyed the parts that could be easily fixed. All the techy stuff - the finicky, expensive, labour-intensive bits - remained untouched.

The Other Side had done the same all over the City. The power plant, hospitals, medical labs, even the bus depot; every valuable facility had been isolated by wreckage. He figured the Enemy had used the same strategy right across the Country, since it had worked so well. As Grampa would have said of their process, 'Why fix it if it ain't broke?'

The bus reached Oakmont Drive. Someone with a sense of humour had spray painted a '55' on the speed limit sign. The bus, straining to attain the highway speed of 25, lurched and shuddered its way down the homestretch to his subdivision. Jack resumed his inspection of the brochure. Sophie had found it on their front doorknob, stapled to a complimentary white hand towel.

Its cover bore a suburban scene in living color. Cotton-ball clouds posed against a childishly blue sky; sunshine lit a comb-straight street bristling with driveways. You could almost hear the lawnmowers, smell the back-yard grills. On the closest driveway were two members of a Removal Crew, dressed like old-time mattress delivery men, white coveralls and blue disposable booties. They loaded canned goods into a crisp white cube van.

At the edge of the picture, a kindly looking man in a white lab coat held paperwork out for signature to a man and woman. The couple appeared long ill-used, worn down by worry and desperation. 'Rode hard and put away wet,' as Grampa used to say.

The husband, though, had hope blooming upon his face. Looking like he just found a brand-new source of salvation, he reached eagerly for the Doctor's pen. The wife leaned in, peering past her man to see the contract, strangling a towel with both hands, her knuckles as white as the cloth.

In gold script, the name of the company flowed across the glossy paper: Dr. K's Euthanasia Removals. "Call Dr. K's and Rest in Peace… Lowest Minimums in the Business!"

Jack glanced up from the brochure and caught a look from another passenger. She sat, placidly jiggling with the bus' motion, comfortably overflowing one of the sideways-facing seats. Jack hadn't seen such a rich person in a long time. He watched, fascinated at such excess, as the bus hit potholes and the resulting bumps sent ripples across the skin of her cheeks and chins. She must be incredibly wealthy. She didn't seem stuck up about it, though, which was nice. She scrutinized him in turn, taking all of him in: he was made up of knees and elbows, cheekbones and pointy chin. And ribs. Shoulder blades and ribs. Clearly, Jack was not in the same 1% category as this lady. Must be nice, to carry around so many riches, so much security.

"My sister Debra went with Dr. K's," she said, gesturing at the brochure. "Debbie never had had much meat on her bones, she knew she wouldn't last long. She must've had something stashed, though, or how else could she afford them?"

"Oh," Jack said. "How were they? I mean, uh…"

"I don't know," the woman shrugged. "You know how it is, friends and family aren't allowed to be there. But they must have done their job right because Debbie's not there any more, either."

Jack nodded. He got off at the next stop, walking home on autopilot, still reading. The brochure had a lot of whats and whys, but few hows. He checked again, then found a small section entitled "Methodology." No details, just a blurb about a 'variety of safe methods.' *Who gives a shit about 'safe'?* He wondered. People wouldn't worry about infection or side effects, accidental addictions or allergies. They would be wanting effective. Efficient. Thorough. Painless and/or fast. And guaranteed – definitely guaranteed. Guaranteed would be good. *'Safe' assisted suicide? Fucking marketing bullshit!*

Bullshit that people wanted to believe in. Nobody knew how to deal with the culture shock of the last couple of years. Countries stepped upon allies to fawn over former foes. The United Nations and NATO disbanded. Immigrants and refugees were detained or outlawed, then shot. Bullish stock markets, driven by war-hungry speculators, stampeded. The dollar, abandoned by foreign investors, crashed. Hyper-inflation, like a blimp that's slipped its moorings, floated, unchecked and inevitable, beyond retrieval. And when the Enemy sent bombs into North American back yards, part of our collective psyche simply packed up and went home.

We all thought we could handle it. We thought we could model WWI Brits, and 'Keep Calm and Carry On', but, actually: no. Or, like Churchill, we would never surrender, but, after all: no. We swore no one would be left behind, but again: no. And when we tired of it, or ran out of food, hope and sanity, we expected to calmly dispatch themselves - and our loved ones - with the same level of cold efficiency we used to see in the movies: no.

The Weapons Drive hadn't helped the public, either. Government Clean-Up Crews had gone on a house-to-house, door-to-door round-up. Honesty and responsibility had ensured that most citizens donated their weaponry, and with no firearms, what were people supposed to do, get out the baseball bat? A twig? Grampa would have had a lot to say about the need to pry his rifle from his cold, dead fingers. He would have been pleased with Jack. His grandson hadn't turned in all of his hunting gear, not by a long shot.

Removal companies like Dr. K's were the brutally logical answer to this kaleidoscope of horrors. Many people tried to do it themselves; that never seemed to work out well. One of Jack's friends from work tried the murder-suicide route. He had missed his wife, shot right through the apartment wall, got the next-door lady by mistake. Others botched things, maiming themselves or loved ones. Even Dominic, the local paramedic who saved that kid last Halloween, had messed it up. Having only ingested enough poison to paralyze himself, he starved to death in his mostly full kitchen.

Almost home, Jack heard the unmistakable sound of a party winding down, coming from one of the garages up ahead. Brad, who used to serve on the Community Council with Jack, waved him over. He and Ginger were having a "Can't Take it With You" Bash. Ginger had registered the two of them with a slave trader.

"Just don't leave it too late, man," Brad said, handing Jack a warm beer, "that's what happened to us. We were rationing, but suddenly we didn't have enough food left to pay a Removal Company. They always talk about low minimums, but it was still more than we had. Then we tried to do it ourselves, but we couldn't go through with it. So we called a Trader." He checked his watch. "They should be here pretty soon, actually, Ginger went inside to finish packing up."

Jack took a swig of his beer, said, "I noticed Kim and her mom had a white sheet flying on their flag pole."

"That oughta get a Removal Crew's attention! Lotta people have thrown in the towel lately."

"Yeah, remember those people who used to run that East Indian restaurant? Rani? With all those daughters? I heard her guy – what's her husband's name again, Muhammed?"

"Mo."

"Right. Mo spent all his goods taking care of them, then he had to join a Crew. Was really expensive, Removal services for five people, but he said he wasn't risking it, said there was no way he was letting Traders have his wife and daughters." As soon as Jack said the words, he thought of Ginger and he wondered when he would learn to shut the hell up. "I'm sure he was just being paranoid, Brad."

"Well, I got quotes from three Traders, you know, and they have to sign a Usage contract…" Brad said.

"Exactly," Jack said, "I've seen the ads, they are legally bound by the terms of your contract, and there's that new protective legislation… You guys will be fine."

The Trader arrived before Ginger did, in a black pick-up truck with a matching cargo canopy. Hazard lights flashing, the truck backed into the driveway, set the emergency brake.

A bearded dude in a black leather vest came out with a clipboard, checked Brad's ID and ticked his name off the list. Sizing Jack up, he asked, "How about you, man? You good?"

“Yeah,” Jack said, thinking of their diminishing stores, carefully split into various caches around the house. Sophie was all about asset management; she kept a token stockpile in the kitchen, readily visible, but squirreled the rest. Too many people had been in their house, seen their treasures, whatever food they had on hand. Seen Jack’s enticing wife. Jack had a stockpile that not even Sophie knew about, though. His old Army gear bag held a rifle, ammunition and enough meds to allow them to literally pick their poison, should it come to that. Jack agreed with his grandfather, when he had said, ‘If you want something done right, do it yourself.’

“Good to hear,” the guy said. “Here’s one of my cards, in case you change your mind. People gotta eat, right?”

Ginger came out wiping her eyes and adjusting her backpack. She kept her jaw clenched and sunglasses on while hugging Jack, said, “Give Sophie a hug for me, love you guys.” She walked up to the back passenger-side door.

The driver shook his head, pointed behind them, said something inaudible.

“Pardon?” Ginger said.

The guy in the vest unlocked the canopy door, folded down the tailgate.

“In the back,” the driver yelled. “Slaves ride in the back!”

Serious as a Heart Attack

By Lynne Zotalis

In April, journaling, I wrote this to my husband (he'd been dead for 17 years)

Well, Chuck, I'm trying so hard to keep everything together. Very hard. I believe I'm doing well, making a go of it, a good show and still the gnawing persistence of 'now what, or what else or what if' echoes and haunts as if some force may, might, could overtake me and I'll make a misstep, huge or miniscule but nonetheless thwarting. When can I BE CONFIDENT? When is it MY TIME? Help me be strong, Chuck. Give me faith and doggedness to stay the course—don't give in. The eagle soaring overhead today, a sign that you are seeing, upholding and undergirding. Leading me on. I have raised my kids, our four kids, I'm done with the full time go-to babysitter, cleaner, all around assistant. I'll make an orderly and determined transition to the next chapter and I don't even think it's the final one. I've got a lot of productivity in me and it's going to be successful.

So, goodnight, my love, be in my dreams, heart and soul. Forever. Onward.

* * *

Mid July.

It could always get worse, be worse and guess what? IT DID! Jesus H Christ. The test of mettle, yet again. Now I have coronary heart disease. One strong chest pain episode 2 weeks ago. Chewed 2 aspirin and it went away in 20 minutes. That was weird, I thought, not knowing what to make of it having never experienced anything akin. I work out. I eat right. I'm at an ideal weight. I'm too healthy for it to be… *that*.

Then, Monday night, I had another pain, twice as bad and long. I debated whether to call 911 for the entire hour. I guess I should have, in hindsight, but it's really hard to make that decision. For one thing, I wasn't in my hometown; I was 150 miles away, in a motel. So what would happen to my stuff, my car, where would they take me? Doing nothing more strenuous than working on a writing project, it hit instantly, crushing. Unable to move from my chair, slightly bent over, I couldn't straighten up or take a deep breath or I envisioned my chest literally exploding. I was able to roll the office chair to my bag where I had 4 aspirin, which I chewed, repeating 'this is not going to kill me, be calm, be Zen, don't panic.' It will pass. I don't *know* it's a heart attack. It could be but I don't think it is and maybe if I don't acknowledge it and Chuck, you need to help me. Don't let me die. Come on, be here. With me. Now. This can't be IT. I sat inert taking the shallow breaths and it abated enough for me to get to the bed and lie down. I took half a Xanax and felt relief as I dozed off.

In the morning with a dull ache in my chest it seemed manageable enough to drive home. I'd be better off in my surroundings, I thought; my medical system, my support network. Driving out of Minneapolis I surmised if it hits hard again I'll pull into Southdale Fairview hospital, the same for Rochester, but it seemed alright. It did. I plowed southward three hours, driving straight to the ER entrance of my local hospital. That's when it ramped into over-drive. 'I don't know if I should go to urgent care or the ER,' I told the receptionist and she asked, 'What's happening?' When I said chest pain, it was ON! Gurney, staff running, needles, EKG, chest X-ray, meds.

Twice they asked me if anyone was with me. The second time I explained that my partner thinks I'm out of town so when you call him you're going to have to make sure he understands I'm here, at this hospital. Scott arrived in minutes. The verdict was a transport by ambulance to Mayo in LaCrosse, Wisconsin, 70 miles away. At this point I knew my kids needed to be informed so I asked Scott to call my oldest daughter. 'Do you want to tell her,' he asked. 'No, I'll cry,' I answered. He said, 'Well, then I'll cry too.' She was tasked with calling her 3 siblings, our standard chain of command.

What a horribly raucous ride bumping my pain level from 3 to 7, you know, how they always say rate your discomfort with those digressing smiley faces from 1 to 10. Ridiculous. It was like riding in a tank. Which I've never done but I imagined. It was mid afternoon by the time I was wheeled into the cardiac unit in LaCrosse. An echo cardiogram and heart catheterization would have to wait until the next morning, I assume because my symptoms weren't life threatening. My son arrived, speeding 3 hours from Minneapolis to wait, to lend much needed courage to this freaked out mom.

90% of this is likely attributed to my father's DNA, him having severe heart disease as well as his maternal side pretty much all dying in their early 50s. My life style is such that I couldn't do any more to ameliorate this. It would have progressed to a major heart attack that I most likely wouldn't have survived. So I'm lucky? The only thing that I'd noticed over the past 2 years was that I had to work harder to get a deep yoga breath, raising my shoulders while inhaling. I thought it was normal. It wasn't typically what you'd call short of breath. It didn't dawn on me it was anything more than aging. My symptoms were gradual over an indefinite amount of time and years. My cardiologist's comment, 'You can't cheat genetics.'

At noon I was wheeled into the cath lab where it was explained, they'd go up through my arm, first with a camera, then a balloon to open anything up and then stents placed if required. Or worst case, if too many blockages were found or they were too profound; they'd stop the procedure, having to transport me to either Rochester or EauClaire where said surgery would be performed. All of the prepping was extremely detailed, garnering my consent, understanding that if my heart stopped, YES, I wanted to be revived. That was the final question and they wheeled me into the OR. It was all of 59 degrees, me, naked with a thin drape, my teeth chattering so hard, I was shaking so intensely I thought, how will they keep me immobile? With some great medication, that's how. Valium, Benedryl, Versed and Fentanyl. Oh yeah! It's called conscious sedation in order to inform the surgeon of extreme pain or to respond to his request, say, if you need to take a deep breath and hold it. Above and to my left there was an enormous screen that televised the process which I declined to watch. I knew what was going on but I didn't care. Drugs are amazing. How they can go from your wrist up through an artery threading it precisely into your heart? Mind blowing. At the end of the procedure, at the catheter site, a tourniquet type clamp was placed around my wrist, pumped up to such intensity for several hours until the blood clotted. But this made the blood pool around the top and bottom in my hand and up my arm so that the nurses had to press as hard as they could in order to disperse *this* blood and prohibit it from coagulating. Excruciating.

My heart required two stents in my right coronary artery. Two 80% blockages. Synergy stents, known for their enhanced capacity to deliver medication for three months preventing platelets from attaching and clogging up the new opening. Sent home the following morning, I am disbelieving, boggled. Did this really happen?! Incredulous to have these two metal tubes in my very heart improving my circulation, pumping blood and oxygen to my body, my brain.

Now the meds, which I'm trying to get regulated, staggering doses trying to circumvent the goddamn woozy, weird, nauseous side effects. My arm is alright as long as I don't bend it or twist it, bruising is on-going, spreading from wrist to shoulder, getting more colorful daily reminding me of the ordeal, the seriousness. Scott was a rock, so steady, calm, centered. I keep trying to wrap my head around it; Tuesday, Wednesday and Thursday they released me. BOOM. I'm focused and absorbed in this recovery. My kids got such a fright with the possibility of losing me, their last parent. It makes me so sad to contemplate such a possibility. My daughter, her husband, and my granddaughter drove three hours, ready to take over, at once doing everything, treating me like an invalid, which I have to be okay with. Shut up and let them be helpful, loving, kind. I'm doing as well as I am because of their generosity and support.

Anxiety pounces. I freak. Sleep arrives after Xanax. It will straighten out, mellow out. I'll adjust. Friends are extremely loving with offers to do anything, everything. I choke up at their benevolence and am sad I've caused this hearts' wrenching; so confusing and intense.

I'm up to walking around the block 3 times a day and will talk to a physical therapist to begin rehab when my arm stops hurting. After seeing the cardiologist today, less than a week later, the Crestor is cut by half, also blood pressure half to alleviate the achy lightheadedness and joint pain. I have never taken medication and really hate it so this is going to be a challenge. He explained how the heart and arteries don't like to be messed with so they rebel, spasm. But they don't warn you or arm you with this knowledge. Probably because of the power of suggestion. I'd wake in the night with such severe pain, the only remedy was to soak in an Epsom salt bath. No matter what hour.

Now, 'fix me so this will never happen again' has become my new mantra. That will make it all worthwhile. I will get my strength and mobility back; be fit and vibrant. Life is valuable and precious. I do believe I already knew this but definitely, more so now.

A good friend with a similar experience told me to watch for depression. The doctors don't tell you that either but it's quite common especially given my sleep deprivation. He said, in one of a dozen pep talks, to be mindful and grateful for intervention and medication that makes me one of the lucky ones. I'll try.

It will take some time, some reflection and a lot of patience and possibly I won't ever be able to say, 'Things are back to normal.' But it is my choice, it is up to me how I will proceed with my life, my diet, my regimen, my attitude. I am humbled. The rug has been pulled out from under me and I've done some deep soul searching trying to glean the lessons this is teaching. It feels different. I do. Change has occurred in an instant making me more thoughtful, wizened, grateful. Alive. So this is what they mean by 'serious as a heart attack'? Duly noted.

George

by Trevor Maynard

George was born like a bullet!

One minute rolled up with his siblings: like little pigs in blankets, his blood pulsing with oxygen and nutrients from his mother, one of his brothers buried deeper along the womb, queuing behind; the next, squeezed, squashed, and catapulted into the world, a damp ball of fur with one ear raised. Misty, his mother, gave a low howl, and then seemed to hiccup, but not a human sound of that kind, more an interrupted purring. She roughly licked George, licking him again, and again, as his body and legs unfurled, then his tail and finally his other ear sprang free. His eyes remained tightly shut.

We, Mary and I, watched where once there was one and now there were two; not an unusual sight for Mary, who as a midwife had delivered eighteen human babies in the last fortnight alone and had previously bred both cats and dogs on a semi-professional basis; but for me, this was my first, and it was a complete wonder. George was an impressive butterfly patterned tabby with the addition of four white socks, a nuzzle of white around his chin, and two white smears through both his eyebrows. He resembled an old man, but not just any old man, one old man in particular: my paternal grandfather, who seasonally worked as a department store Santa, and for whom he was now named.

'Grandpop', as me and my brother knew him, was a very tall, upright man, always immaculately dressed, whose hazel brown eyes had dimmed a little since his Renee's passing, but as he might have said "better to be remembering than remembered." To him, I felt sure, I was a weird kid. I like Shakespeare, hence my flowery reminiscence. I like the stars – Jupiter and Saturn as well as the Starsky and Hutch type, and I write poetry.

Once, when I was six years old, I remember him towering above me as I went to ask him a question. My hands were, as per my usual, tightly held down by my side, with two fingers from each hand tucked under each thumb and I looked straight up - straight up his nostrils and, trying not to get distracted by his profusion of nose hairs that held a well grown bogie in place, I asked him what a Zen garden was.

"It's a … " He ventured after a long pause, and then smiled. "Would you like a boiled sweet, me'boy?" He indicated the multi-coloured collection in clear wrappers in the now re-appropriated (since his third heart attack) ashtray. "Renee, what's a Zen Garden?" He asked. My grandmother handed him the gardening book I had been looking at for the past half an hour. "Ah," he laughed heartily, like a Father Christmas might have.

Misty was resting now, after her first exertions, only she being aware of whether any more kittens were in there – well George possibly knowing of at least one: a carbon copy of his mother in the mode of *Felix*, the best known of all black and white cats. But for now, George's paws were pushing and paddling at Misty's bulbous white belly finding one of several pink protruding teats, dense with milk. Totally blind, he instinctively suckled on, but lost grip and soon slid off, tumbling, more rodent than feline, like a furry, misshapen chipolata. Not for long though, he grabbed, pushed, and paddled his way back, to a different teat as his mother meowed and panted: labouring on. We gave Misty praise, strokes of encouragement, congratulations and soft words, Mary thinking maybe there were three more: one more from the left uterus, and two from the right …

"Yes, Pete, of course cats have two. A lot of animals do, how do you think they have so many young at once?" She chided me gently, her eyes slightly downcast in that coy yet knowing way. I pondered for a moment, extrapolating what this might mean for mice and guinea pigs, how many uteruses might they have, but my train of thought was derailed by a further sharp meowl from Misty. The mother cat, standing and turning, George being thrown left, then down, and now was stuck underneath her. Mary rescued him and delicately steered Misty around to wait for her next contraction. The black and white kitten, given the misnomer Boston because of four white socks (even though the actual baseball team is called the Boston Red Socks) squeezed out; followed shortly by a smoky grey and white fluff ball, to be called, unsurprisingly, Smokey; and finally Fred, a tinier, little runt version of George but with the only white being two back socks and in a tiger tabby style: his stripes strikingly straight, like the big cat.

Many may ask, but what of the father? What of George the Cat's Dad? Well, therein lies a tale. George would meet him soon, as soon as Misty was later back in heat, a suitable gap after this litter's birth. Misty had several suitors, who lined up on the wall and, if in with a chance, on the fallen tree trunk in our back garden, in front of the kitchen window. There was a beautiful, long haired, lion of a tom, with smoky blue fur among swatches of white. His face was white apart from a patch of grey above his left eye and the whole of his nose. He was the cat to whom we, Mary and I, aspired to wish for as father of her kittens.

Then there was a ginger cat, a *Marmalade* if ever one should be called, with a flat face and yellow eyes, who stared intently, then fell asleep. There were three others, but of little consequence, as they were way too far down the pecking order. Then there was the prime candidate who wasn't the fleetest of foot but with the best sob story it would seem. He was a scruffy moggy of indeterminate colour, slightly thinner than he should be, and with a pronounced limp of the left hind leg. It was almost as if the others with great sympathy seemed to say – “alright mate, go on, you first” ... It was he who inevitably triumphed to plant his seed.

George, six months old, and twice the size of his siblings, eyed this interloper with cursing jade eyes, slit through the middle with deep jett black; his ears bent down and back in threat, his tail tip flicking high in agitation. George’s Dad, appeared to nod, might it be said admiringly? Maybe. Nonchalantly? For sure. Then sauntered away, three paws, hop, three paws, hop, three paws, hop. George’s Mum, back on heat now, awaiting her prospective new bloom and brood, would have to wait for another day.

George now had an established tuft of white on his chin, and walked tall with a long swaying gait, his strong, thick tail perpendicular to his back, and with just the tip occasionally flicking. His white chest was puffed out and there was a pride and strength in his stare. Much like my grandfather in many details except maybe one; George appeared to be a very gay cat. It has been said that if you name a person, or an animal, for a person, they will in some way come to inherit that person’s persona; they, of course, also say, that that person, or animal, will also develop their own individual twist. And so it had become with George: he was definitely a bit of a joker.

Earlier, several years earlier, after five trips to America in three years, my Grandfather had found himself in a snowstorm at John F Kennedy Airport in New York under the watchful eye of U.S. Immigration and Custom Officers. He was seventy-eight years old, could only walk a hundred yards due to his heart condition, but was now being classed as an illegal immigrant because he had outstayed his visitor's visa. He was also thought to be wearing a Father Christmas beard. Not that he was officially being deported, but it made a better story for Grandpop to imply that he was. One of the officers had thought the beard fake, and actually pulled it, then, apparently, the whole atmosphere had lightened as Grandpop had told them he was only at the airport because his reindeers were snowed in at Chicago. You see, Grandpop George was a right old character.

"Hello boy, you alright boy?" His best Southend accent bellowed into my answerphone. "A cat? Named a cat after me? Nice one, boy. Nice one. Good. Moss!.. (my auntie's nickname)" – his loud voice drifted away from the receiver as he spoke to her, affirming the cat was named after him. "Well, see yer then, boy. See yer! Goodbye." Across the ether there was a sound like something snapping, or cracking, and then falling with a dull thud. The line was still open, a siren blared, and then the distant talking to my aunt, before she picked up the receiver and spoke. "Peter, Grandpop's pulled the phone off the wall, clumsy old sod!" But she wasn't angry, in fact she was laughing. We all knew Grandpop's talent for clumsiness, legend in our clan. "Pete? Pete? Oh!...It's an ans'aphone, Dad!" – then her voice became distant as she spoke away from the receiver. "Dad! It's an ans'aphone! It's a message! He isn't in." Her deep, smoked soaked, slightly Americanised voice returned. "Ok, Sweetie. I'll talk to you later. My love to your Mum and Dad, and you and Mary." A kiss, then – beep – *end of message.*

George the Cat, Little Fred (his name now amended) and Misty sat in a line on the windowsill, looking out at us as we returned. Boston, now called Oliver, lived in Esher, whilst his brother, Smokey, had departed for Brighton, his new appellation unknown. Misty had since had two more litters. The most recent being Molly and Chloe, two silky, grey, low slung and slightly podgy felines whose body shape mimicked their mother's, though they themselves would not go on to give birth, and Smudge and Fudge, two predominantly white cats, with saddle patches of tortoiseshell tabby. These latter four would remain with us and were now six weeks old, living in a cardboard box, their curiosity of the outside world, and the presence of older siblings, driving them to distraction.

George sat fully upright, chest puffed out, his face longer, more mature, sleek like the revered felines painted on Egyptian vases. He also seemed to know this. Little Fred copied the posture, but he wasn't quite tall enough, long enough, or stocky enough, and anyway he was that bit too much excited to sit still for two minutes. Misty slumped down, half asleep, tired, glad to be free until her next feeding session, and I'm sure, finally compelling me and Mary to keep any further suitors away. Being humans, however right or wrong it may be, we would help her with a short trip to the vets. There would be no more kittens, and her suitors would lose interest. And we, being humans, once the kittens were weaned, made that choice for her.

Grandpop's funeral had been a solemn affair; well, not actually all that solemn really. Yes, we were all sad, but he had lived to eight-five, twenty-nine years after the first of eight heart attacks, and ten years longer than his Renee. He had stayed independent, with the aid of an electric chariot, two tireless daughters-in-law, the love of his sons, grandchildren and greatgrandchildren, and the frequent anticipation of his trips to the States to see his daughter. His namesake lazily circled one ear with a paw, then the other, determinedly watching us as we exited the car in our suits and black ties, having never met the human George, but becoming more like him with every breath, I was glad I had named him for my grandfather. Little Fred was at the door to greet us, but George just tilted his head, his whiskers many and white, seemingly random, flickering in the light.

I had spoken at my grandmother's funeral and my brother's wedding, and now again, at Grandpop's departure. My dad's best friend suggested I should do the whole circuit, weddings, funerals, christenings, bar mitzvahs, birthdays, corporate do's. "You'd make a bomb!" He enthused. Well, I had 'em laughing, if not in the aisles, then chortling in the pews at the cremation, as I reminded everyone of the time Grandpop had "*acquired*" a number of miniature carriage clocks in his last stint as a department store Santa, which he liberally distributed to friends and family for the discount rate of £1 (£5 to punters).

I can still hear his spiel. The patter did not diminish with age. ...*"Guaranteed to tell the exact time at least twice a day, Christmas and Bank Holidays, come rain or shine, hail and thunder, no matter which country or time zone you are in. Ideal for birthdays, mothers' days, holidays, by appointment to the King, the Queen, the Jack, in fact, the whole deck of cards!"...* We all had tears in our eyes and laughter in our hearts, as, per his wishes, the passage of his coffin from this world was accompanied by the strains of *Match of the Day*.

Sitting outside on Grandpop's memory bench, eyes closed, contemplating recent events, it seemed barely five minutes since I'd read my grandmother's book and my grandfather had given me that boiled sweet. The garden now gloriously bathed in the warm spring sunshine, mine and George's favourite time of year; I close my eyes and turn my face up to meet the sun. Distant traffic gives way to sparrow and thrush, and a chatty robin skips to a higher branch as I sense George padding purposefully alongside me on the seat.

I feel his comforting, majestic energy, chest puffed out and tail proudly high. I feel him nuzzle my back, before he sits beside me, and I remember how he'd been born like a bullet and we named him for my grandfather; in what seems the fleetest of time, we are, today, naming this memory garden for the passing of our wonderful, beloved cat, George.

It has a small and ever flowing stream, always cool and always clear, which flows across flat grey stones and under a small wooden bridge, proportionate in size for a cat to cross. In turn this leads to a Chinese style house no more than two feet high; before it a rock pool where a steam outlet creates an illusion of mist rolling across the surface, swirling around the figure of a cat, carved in black granite, curled up in a peaceful sleeping position; and finally, mounted between the apex of the eaves of the little house there is a miniature carriage clock which reads ten minutes to two, as it always has and always will, such is our perfect little Zen garden.

BIOGRAPHIES

Piet Pedersson

Written under the pen name Piet Pedersson, to reflect his Scandinavian origins, the writer is an author of novels and poetry.

Meanwhile, writing fan fiction and adult content elsewhere, he is published widely in online magazines and blogs.

He has four children, lives in England, and enjoys running and motor racing.

Gregg Voss

Gregg Voss is a marketing communications writer during the day and covers high school sports most evenings and weekends. In the intervening time, he is a prolific fiction writer, with work that has appeared in publications as diverse as The Write Launch, Red Fez and Door County Magazine.

Additionally, he released his first short story collection, The Valley of American Shadow, on July 4, 2019. He is also working on a second short story collection and a novel.

Kevin Michael Patrick

Kevin is a American born writer living in Spain who spent many years in the magical city of London.

His flights of fancy have also taken in New York and Sydney, and though twice divorced, he is a firm believer in romance.

This is a true story, and Claire is the real name of his first wife, though his name is a pen name.

Mike Friers

Mike Friers is a bit of a petrol head and has written for several online blogs on Formula 1 and Touring Cars - this is his first attempt at fiction.

He is 46, lives in Essex with his daughter Mel, his son Chris, and his dog Sheba.

He is currently working on a novel based in and around his childhood.

Teri Bran

Teri Bran is a British born Australian content writer living in the UK with his two children and a dog named Sam.

His work often involves nostalgia and childhood memories; and has been published in the Garan Review, New South Wales Times, and various online blogs and webpages.

However, this is only his second story to have been placed in a competition, the last was when he was aged seven and was also about his next door neighbour.

Dean Gessie

Dean Gessie is a Canadian writer who has won multiple international prizes for his poetry and fiction, including first prize for his short story in the prestigious 'Half and One Prize' in India.

Dean also won the Bacopa Literary Review Short Story Contest in Florida and he won second prize (of more than 2000 submissions) in the Short Story Project New Beginnings competition in New York.

Additionally, Dean was chosen for inclusion in The Sixty Four Best Poets of 2018 by Black Mountain Press in North Carolina. He has also published three novellas with Anaphora Literary Press in Texas.

R.D. Girvan

A banker by day/writer by night, R.D. Girvan recently earned her University of Toronto Creative Writing Certificate. She writes suspense and horror fiction from rural Alberta, Canada.

She is pleased to have been twice-published in STORGY Magazine and accepted for 2019 publication in Coffin Bell Journal.

Facebook: https://www.facebook.com/rdgirvan

Website: https://rdgirvan.com/

Twitter: https://twitter.com/RDGirvan

Lynne Zotalis

As a freelance contributor and member in the Iowa Poetry Association, Lynne's poetry has been published in Lyrical Iowa for eleven years running.

She is a member of the Peace and Social Justice Writers Group at the Loft Literary Center, Minneapolis, MN, with contributions to their chapbook, ***Peace Begins*** and the anthology ***Turning Points: Discovering Meaning and Passion in Turbulent Times.***
Lynne's book ***Saying Goodbye to Chuck*** is a poignantly directed work dealing with the sudden death of her husband, available on Amazon.

The children's book, ***Kenny and Sylvia's Day Out***, championing kindness toward all, was written and illustrated by Lynne.
Her poetry has appeared in various publications including **writing in a woman's voice**, ***Tuck Magazine*** and ***The Poetic Bond VII and VIII.***
Reading selected works this year at Common Ground gallery, Silver City, NM is posted on YouTube.

Lynne's stories have won publication in the Cunningham Short Story Competition for the third consecutive year, in the books ***Life Dances, Our World, Your Place*** and ***Nine Frames.***

Trevor Maynard

Editor of the Cunningham Short Story Anthologies ***Life Dances (2017)*** and ***Our World, Your Place (2018),*** Trevor Maynard started his writing career with a series of poetry pamphlets printed off an old Roneo printer, and distributed to family, friends and work colleagues.

After reading Drama and Theatre Studies at *Royal Holloway College, University of London,* he spent ten years writing, directing and producing plays, publishing four one act plays in ***Four Truths,*** as well as the plays ***GLASS,*** and ***From Pillow To Post.***

In 2009, his first poetry collection was published ***Love, Death, and the War on Terror***, followed by ***Keep on Keepin' On*** in 2012, and ***Grey Sun, Dark Moon*** in 2015.

Trevor has been the editor of the international poetry anthology series ***The Poetic Bond*** since 2011 and will publish ***The Poetic Bond IX*** in late 2018. So far, ***The Poetic Bond*** has showcased the work of 214 poets from 32 countries.

Publications featuring his work include **Aesthetica, Tuck, October Hill, Deep Underground, Poetry, Life and Times**, **Miracle,** and the anthology **Men in the Company of Women (EAP)**.

Trevor is a member of **The Poetry Society (UK)** and formerly an executive member of **The Writer's Guild of Great Britain**, and treasurer of **The Theatre Writers' Union.**

Our World Your Place

ISBN-10: 1727650689 / ISBN-13: 978-1727650686

Featuring the winners of The Cunningham Short Story Competition, 2019.

"Veiled" by Rebecca Evans - Two women, centuries apart, dance a dance of seven veils to save the world.

"The Seal" by Rebekah Dodson - People were unkind to the girl who grew up a seal, but one day her prince will come

"The Bench" by Karen Quinnon - A mother of two, her younger party-girl sister, and a question she must ask

"Of Strange Lands and People" by James Najarian - Brendan and Garo, an Armenian-American gay couple search for Brendan's birth father

"Slim" by Tonya Walker - an imagined tale of a pregnant Slim Keith, second wife of film director, Howard Hawks

"Sentenced to Life" by Oscar Heitmart - Future Earth: it is your right to die at thirty, break the law - you will be sentenced to life

"The Viet Kieu Casanova" by Tuan Phan - A Vietnamese-American returns 'home' as a certain kind of 'tourist'

"The World I Grew Up In" by Lynne Zotalis - the innocence of a 'fifties childhood in Wisconsin does not mean there is not tragedy.

The competition was won by Rebecca Evans, for which she received a prize of $100.

Life Dances

ISBN-10: 1978098030 / ISBN-13: 978-1978098039

To honour the life of his grandfather, **Robert Hamilton Cunningham,** in 2017, Trevor Maynard set up a short story competition, the theme of which was for each story to open the reader's eyes to the wider world we live.

RH Cunningham travelled the world, initially with The Royal Navy during World War II, and later as a Chief Steward on cruise liners. He was a bit of a storyteller, with a fair singing voice, and an always interesting perspective on life. In his 'seventies, he began to reflect on his life in a series of long hand journals which were later transcribed by his son RF Cunningham, and then adapted into a short story, ***The Dance,*** by his grandson.

The competition was won by **Sandy Norris** with her story "**No Going Back",** for which she received a prize of $100. The five runners-up were **Maria Borland** "Baking", **Linda DuPret** "When Food Kills", **Michael McLaughlin** "The Death of Rock'n'Roll", **Israela Marglait** "Too Much" and **Lynne Zotalis** "True North".

"As an eclectic collection of short stories, exploring humanity, and its place in the world, this neat little anthology, delivers an interesting read."
KD (Utah, USA)

"Trevor Maynard's "The Dance" provides a fascinating, honest and personal window into life during the war years and is equally matched by the short stories the competition set up around it inspired."
RM (Glasgow, UK)

Further Details available at www.willowdownbooks.com

Grey Sun, Dark Moon

A collection of poems by Trevor Maynard

This collection of poetry hovers around the shadows of melancholy, occasionally rising to joy, often falling to darkness. It is an intimate study of the frailties of life, the human condition. Symbolically, the passage of time is explored, from Sunrise to Morning, then Later, Dusk to Night.

SUNRISE, new life, the growing of awareness, the innocence of love MORNING, change, the first half of life, time passes LATER, the afternoon of existence, the coming of old age, the nature of being DUSK, man in society, the violence of politics, the place of Man in Nature NIGHT, the human condition, tragic narratives, the reality of love.

A day's passing, echoing the movement of life through time, questioning; what unites us, in meaning and experience, as our days pass, life ruthlessly ticking away; how does this modern existence relate to the natural world around us?

"Trevor B Maynard combines complicated thematic material and unites fractured images with a sure hand." (THE STAGE)

The author's previous poetry collections are KEEP ON KEEPIN' ON (2012) and LOVE, DEATH AND THE WAR ON TERROR (2009).

Echoes in the Earth

A collection of poems by Pushpita Awasthi, edited by Trevor Maynard

ISBN:-10 1533618801, ISBN:-13 978-1533618801

Through the twin themes of Nature and Love, ***Echoes and the Earth*** not only illuminates humanity as a whole but the individual's own human relationship with the human world. These elements of being human are skilfully interwoven, creating a poetic expression that has depth, articulates understanding, and possesses empathy.

It is a work that swirls with energy: darting and surprising, leaping and resting, comforting and challenging - a spiritual, philosophical, and human journey.

The Watcher from the Beacon

Poetry by Peter Alan Soron
edited by Trevor Maynard

ISBN:-10 1480108804, ISBN:-13 978 -1480108806

A collection of poetry from the edge of imagination, where Mankind thrashes against itself, defying logic, embracing logic, both spiritual and reductionist. Sometimes a poem comes from the merest tangent of thought, or a feeling of outrage, sometimes from the ecstasy of love. Now and then it is fully formed, at other times it requires further input from the reader, maybe it tells you something, or avoids telling you anything, and sometimes you can feel the words fall upon your body and seep into your consciousness.

It is poetry of the Human Condition.

The Poetic Bond

The Poetic Bond series of poetry anthologies is now in its ninth year, and has published 213 poets from 30 countries, contributing 514 poems, over seven volumes. Since 2011, including this year, over 1100 poets have submitted nearly 4,500 poems, and while most of the work comes from the US and the UK, there has been an increase in the numbers of entries from India, Canada and Australia.

A shortlist of 56 poets was announced in August, 2019, with at least half of this number expected to be published in The Poetic Bond IX in November 2019.

So, what makes a Poetic Bond?

The process of selecting poems for publication in ***THE POETIC BOND*** series is unlike any other in that there is no set plan as to what will be published. It depends on the themes that emerge from the pool of work submitted, or to put it another way, the poetic energy which comes together at this certain time and place. Where themes emerge, patterns of energy harmonize, form bonds, connections, and these in turn lead to interconnected chapters, and the creation of a holistic volume, deeply connected with humanity, nature, and the universe.

"The poetry that fills this book is moving, deep, and affirming"
Nicholas Chiarkas (WI, USA)
"…very impressed with much of the excellently crafted writing "
Robin Hislop (UK/Spain)
" … a joy to read … thanks for creating this bond and including me in it"
Neetu Malik (PA, USA/India)

The Poets of The Poetic Bond

The Poetic Bond VIII *(2018)*

ISBN-10: 1729531776 ISBN-13: 978 – 1729531778

Victoria Anllo (USA) *Next To / ReSounding /* **Christine Anderes (USA)***: Dead Sea / Confidential /* **Suzanne Askham (UK):** *Upwards / Sulphur Medicine*
Gillian Bell (NZ) *Down on the Beach /* **Annel Bell Martin (USA):** *Watching*
Janette Bendle (AUS) *Enough / Which Way /* **Betty Bleen (USA)** *A Flower's Last Wish / loose threads /* **Joanne Bordokan (CAN)** *Painting /* **Beatrice Huerta Boswell (USA)** *fierce love / Amerigo Verspucci / among the dying / Faith Healing /* **Lexene Burns (AUS):** *Coffee Creates /* **Diane Burrow (UK):** *December /* **Krenare Burqi (Kosovo)** *You /* **Mariangela Canzi (Italy)***: To My Mother /* **Drew Claussen** *Around Life / Bang the Harmonica /* **Ian Colville (UK)** *The Weather Forecast /Imagined Innings of an Old Croft /* **Antonella Corradetti (US)** *My Beauty / Still Love Left In You /* **William DiBenedetto (USA)** *Start Stop /* **Flavia Cosma (CAN)** *Love in the Afternoon / Shipwreck*
Rick Davis (US) *Toxic Personality /* **Bonnie J.Flach (USA):** *You Thought I Never Would /* **Gilbert A.Franke (USA):** *To Be Happy / The House at Prinsengracht 263*
Kelli Gunn (CAN)*:I Know I Promised but … / Season /* **Wybrig de Vries (NL):** *Women with One Lame Hand / Angel /* **Stuart Forrest (USA) /** *Farmers Markets*
Anthony Frobisher (UK) *Summer by the Sea / The Orchard* **Annette Gagliardi (USA)** *Lacuna /* **Bea Garth** *I have never … / Dreaming of Nasturtiums / The Earth as Woman*
Cathryn Glenday (US) *Existential Psychophyics / Twilight Descent / Requiem / Ode to Athena /* **George K Grieve (UK)** *Veracity /* **Karen Henneberry (USA)** *Patriarchy / The ABC's of Womanhood /* **Shari-Jo LeKane-Yetumi (USA)** *After Dark*
KishaJade (UK) *Think Beyond /* **Robin Ouzman Hislop (ESP)***: my cat pi chi / reducto anagrammatico /* **Sebastien Karatonis (USA)** *weight / last laugh for Tina*
Laura Lee (USA) *Click / They left the bed /* **Lee Landau (USA)** *Meeting at the Farmhouse / My Sister Karen Retires* **Madeline Heit Lipton (USA)***: His Name Was James /* **Marek Lugowski (USA)***: Chicago 1993 /* **John McMullen (USA)** *Submission / Why Me?* **Claire Mikkelsen (USA)** *Insouciance /* **Bilal Moin (IND)** *brittle / Happy Hour /* **Karen Nurenberg Rotherstein (USA)** *Oh Me*
Carrie Magness Radna (USA) *Crossing the Border / Pathos / Ashley /*
Bonnie Roberts (USA) *The Bottom of the Sea is Silent / Circus Dwarf /Clues that Melted the Grass / New World Prophecy /* **Sonay Mustafa (IN)** *Do Not Pursue Her*
Reasie Robertson (USA) *Marital Bed … Defiled /* **Biman Roy (IND/USA)** *Picnic Ravisghed / Cat,Jacandar, Shadow* **Trevor Maynard (UK)** *Awaiting the Thunder and Rain / Who I Am /* **Glen Proctor (UK)** *Curtains /***Ivan Saltaric (Croatia)** *Vivid Creation /* **Helen Schulman (USA)** *Stones /***Nancy Scott (USA)** *Still Life with Dead Rabbit and Flugelhorn / The Parade /***Claude Sequy (FR/USA)** *Chimera*
Joseph Sinclair (UK)*: On Firstral Beach / so much joy /* **Richard Glen Smith (USA)** *Jack and Gill Triptych / Shit the Door / Calico Cat and Red Admiral /* **Sarah Stonesifer (USA)** *my regret / Demeter's Plea / 1973-2006 (for Michael) /* **Stephen Sesto (USA)** *Wizen / Inviolatus / Acteon Cry /* **Nana Tokatli (Greece)** *Penelope*
Paul Sutherland (CAN/UK) *Swans on the Witham / Infant Land / The Beloved*
Maria Ivana Treviasani Bach (Italy) *Stretched on the Sand /***Marcia Weber (USA):** *Trees in Winter, Siberia / Lunacy /* **Peter Coe Verbica (USA)** *The Arrest /* **Virus the Poet (USA)** *Colors Pt1 / Direct /* **Kewayne Wadley (USA)** *Non Stop /***Tim Williams (UK)** *Flames Turn to Ash /* **Jim Wilson (US)** *Now /* **Terry Young (USA)** *Bury Me Under the Roses / Touch /***Diane Wend (UK)** *Cold November Moon /* **Marie Youssefirad (USA)** *Somehow /***Cigeng Zhang (China)** *Old Postcard / Father's Old Leather Suitcase*
Lynne Zotalis (USA) *Passage of Years / Cross my Heart*

The Poetic Bond VII *(2017)*

ISBN-10: 1978098030
ISBN-13: 978-1978098039

Christine Anderes (USA): *Slowly / The Oneness / After the rain*
Vesna Adriana Arsenich (USA): *Thought of Two Dimensions / After the Rain*
Suzanne Askham (UK): *Milk of Kindness / Takapuna Beach / Dawn Arrival*
Elaine Battersby (UK): *Voices of Truth* / **Melissa Bird (USA):** *The Stonecutter / Blackhole / I Have Everything* / **Betty Bleen (USA):** *The First Time You Stayed All Night / A Dog Named Seymour / Dancing in the Moonlight*
Lexene Burns (Australia): *Planet Earth / The Ghosts of Time / As I Sleep I Dream*
Diane Burrow (UK): *Sepia Scape / A Spent Cartridge / S.A.D.*
Mariangela Canzi (Italy): *Life / At Night /* **Low Kwai Chee (Malaysia)**: *Nostalgia / Unforgettable You / Happiness* / **Flavia Cosma (Canada):** *I Gathered It All*
Pedro Cuhna (Portugal): *Statement* / **William DiBenedetto (USA)**: *In Love as in War / in my father's step / Poetry of Today* / **Belinda DuPret (UK)**: *Dreaming of Butterflies* / **A.D.Fallon (USA)**: *Elusive Promise / Ambush / Doubt / Hermeneutics of Youth* **Bonnie J.Flach (USA):** *Beyond Oneself / Walk Past /*
Gilbert A.Franke (USA): *A Horizon of Blue / Safe Anchorage* / **Kelli Gunn (Canada)**: *Snake Hunting / 7 a.m.* / **Karen Henneberry (USA)**: *The Emotional Bond / Solace***Robin Ouzman Hislop (UK)**: *Next Arrivals / Abandoned Isle*
Pamela Hope (USA): *Being Free Under Nature's Canopy*
Amber Jimenez-Flores (USA): *These Hands / Do You See As I Do? / A Disharmonious Ode to No Name / You Can Overcome Anything*
Jane Johann (USA): *Layers of Being / The Lone Star / sometimes dark doesn't move .* **Sajida Khan (UK)**: *Silence / Virtual Walls / A Sense of Morality*
Lee Landau (USA): *Ruth's End of Days / Sitting Shiva / Growing Rocks in Ruth's Garden / His Faltering Balance* / **Madeline Lipton (USA)**: *Home, I Hardly Know You* / **Tatjana Loncarec (Croatia)**: *Chosen Memories* / **Annel Bell Martin (USA)** *My Wisteria Vine Swing* / **Kayla Matheson (USA):** *Open Waters* / **Chris Maynard (UK)** : *Dying / Pigeons / Cuddly Cat* /**Trevor Maynard (UK):** *written out / One Minute Late* / **Mustafa Munir (USA)**: *Broken Meditation* /**Deborah Nyamekbe (UK):** *Makola Market Day, Accra Ghana* **Denisa Parsons (USA):** *In Heat / Southern Treasures* / **Lizzie La Poole (UK):** *Have You Ever?* /**Karen Nurenberg Rothstein (USA)**: *Pedro* / **Nancy Scott (USA):** *Gone Fishing / Match Point / Some things Never Change* / **Joseph J.Simmons (USA)**: *Foreign* / **Joseph Sinclair (UK)**: *The Last Apple / A Poet's Supplication* / **Richard Glen Smith (USA):***Reliquary* / **Tom Sterner (USA):** *Cats' Eyes / Creative Survival / The Butterfly Poet* / **Fiona Sullivan (UK):** *Slave / Coming Home / Burnt Black* / **Nana Tokatli (Greece):** *At Home / at times / Attachment Gone* / **Wybrig dr Vries (Netherlands):** *Willows in March / Rain / The Potential To Go Mad is There for Anyone* / **Brian Walker (UK):** *Among the Fragments / My Brother Was Silent /*
Marcia Weber (USA): *Vernal Insurrection / Dreamt Invitation / Overgrowth / Out Eyes Had It* / **Darrell Wright (USA):** *Our End ,,, and Then?* / **Marie Youssefirad (USA):** *Anthropocentric* / **Cigeng Zhang (China):** *I Envy The Butterfly / I Say, You Write* / **Lynne Zotalis (USA)**: *Hey, What Doesn't Kill You / Advice / Solipsist/ Soul Tremors/ A Life in Process*

The Poetic Bond VI (2016)

ISBN-10: 1539334686
ISBN-13: 978-1539334682

Christine Anderes (USA): *The Ossurary of James / The Unquiet Heart*
Pushpita Awasthi (India): *In My Heart of Hearts / Words in the Dark*
Rebecca Behar (France): *Procession*
Betty Bleen (USA): *Grandma 's Jesus / The Cutting Edge*
Diane Burrow (UK): *Speechless / Take a Look at the Hills*
George Carter (UK) *: When I got there* **Diane Colette (US)** : *Fields of Asphodel* ***Ian Coville (UK)*** *: Cliché for our Time / Ploughing*
William DiBenedetto (USA): *time comes uninvited / 7 – May – 1915*
Belinda DuPret (UK): *Isobel* **Amanda Eakins (USA)**: *The Broken Repairman* **Madelina Fine (UK)**: *Lost letter From Love*
Bonnie Flach (USA): *At the Crossroads*
GK Grieve (UK): *The Final Moment Before the Death of Swans / Addict* **Robin Hislop (UK)**: *Tenochitian / In Bed*
Rowland Hughes (UK): *Lemon Soap / A Valley Funeral*
Wendy Joseph (USA): *This is America / In My House, There are Books/ When the Water Rises*
Jill Angel Langlois (USA): *If the Wind Blows / I Remember Silence*
Lawrence W. Lee (USA): *Cynic / Still Life* **Carey Link (USA)** : *8lur Distinctions* **Kwai Chee Low (Malaysia)**: *Cold Winter, Warm Heart*
Neetu Malik (USA) : *dancers / The Pianist / Wanderer*
Trevor Maynard (UK) : *take flight / crushed*
Michael Melichov (Israel) : *Cards*
Miklos Mezosi (Hungary) : *An lamblified Inquiry*
Linda Mills (USA) : *Abide / Winter Seep*
Greg Mooney (USA) : *Insecurities*
Marli Merker Moreira (Brazil) : *Drifters*
Jude Neale (Canada) : *One Cleft Moon*
Hongvan Nguyen (USA) : *Becoming Me*
Bonnie Roberts (USA) : *Cautionary Steps of Love*
George C. Robertson (UK) : *Engraved / A Burning Desire*
Joseph J. Simmons (USA) :*1914*
Nana Tokatfi (Greece) : *Wheat Fields*
Swaizi Vaughan (USA) : *E-Tum Next Left Dead IN / Prepubescent*
Will Walsh (USA) : *Onion Creek, Utah / As I live and breathe / Evolution*
Cigeng Zhang (China) : *Hey, Starting / Special Reunion / Wa Lan / One-line Tide*

The Poetic Bond V (2015)

ISBN-10: 1517783801
ISBN-13: 978-1517783808

Amanda Valerie Judd (USA): Poetry
Belinda Dupret (UK): Ginervra da Benci
Betty Bleen (USA): A Different Mourning
Bonnie Flach (USA): Harbor Night Songs / Realization
Bonnie Roberts (USA): Road Signs.. _/In Vacation Bible School...
Brian McCully (Australia): The Journey of H'won
Caroline Glen (Australia): Together/ Peach Tree
Christine Anderes (USA): Never Sure / Somewhere else...
Cigeng Zhang (China): At 8 'clock / Still For You /
The Moon, The Poet
Claire Mikkelsen (USA): Moa fin' the Blues
Clark Cook (Canada): An Autumn Journey/ Reluctant Travellers
Diane Wend (UK): Sleek in the Sun
Rhona Davidson (UK): Not Just a False Alarm / Waiting/ Stuck
Frances Ayers (USA): Well Fought Tears
Freddie Ostrovskis (UK): The Waiting Tree
Gilbert A. Franke (USA): Music, Love and Memories /
Promises From A Rose Garden
GK Grieve (UK): Jessica / Ian Colville (UK): Group-think
James Sutton (USA): Lenny Bruce Presents J.b
Jill Angel Langlois (USA): Botanical Garden /
Joseph Simmons (USA): lostring / Pete Soron (UK): For Love
Julie Clark (UK): A Babbling Stream / Behold the New Jerusalem
Kewayne Wadley (USA): Together/ Peach Tree
Leander Seddon (Australia): Bird of Paradise,
Linda Mills (USA): Gone Sound / Sleepy Dragon
Marli Merker Moreira (Brazil): Behind Bars
Nana Tokatli (Greece): The white carpet/ an empty space
Neetu Malik (USA): The Cobwebs /A walk in the rain / Limbo
Pushpita Awasthi (Netherlands): Cecile / Synonym of Love
RH Peat (USA): Flying Fingers / The Chinese Restaurant .
Robin Ouzman Hislop (UK): A Split Second Later's Late / The Split
Sonia Kilvington (Cyprus): Wild Montana / Object of Desire
Trevor Maynard (UK): The Grey Sun / Human
Wendy Joseph (USA:) Never Sure / Somewhere else...
William diBenedetto (USA):wow they have

The Poetic Bond IV (2014)

ISBN-10: 1503034526
ISBN-13: 978-1503034525

Christine Anderes *(New York USA) Poem: Illumination*
Mark Beechill *(UK) Poem: Wrangle*
Scott Pendragon Black *(USA) Poem: Past*
Rosalind Brenner *(USA) Poems: The Night Jesus Spoke;*
Art Show; Meeting Mother
Clark Cook *(Canada) Poem: Another Kind of Sunset*
, ***Catherine DeWolf*** *(USA) Poem: Tantrum*
William DiBenedetto *(USA) Poem: 3am overdraft blues*
Belinda Dupret *(UK) Poem: The Scent of Trees*
Bonnie J. Flach *(US) Poem: Najavo Sand Painter*
G A. Franke *(USA) Poem: Reflections on the Sea*
Ingrid Gjelsvik *(Norway) Poems: no frame*
the floe inside the bookcases;
GK Grieve *(UK) Poem Dark Soul*
Peter Hagen *(Norway) Poem: To Set A Big Cry Free*
Seamus Harrington *(Eire) Poems: Free Downloads; Open Day*
Diane Jardel *(Eire) Poem: Alzheimer Blues I & II -*
"It's OK"   " I am here my love"
Trevor Maynard *(UK) Poems: the earthmovers; Clarity*
Clare Mikkelsen *(USA) Poems: A New Bottom Line / Tiny Banker*
Jude Neale *(Canada) Poe: The Arrangement*
Hongvan Nguyen *(USA) Poem: Singers*
RH Peat *(USA) Poems: At The Cost of Others' Eyes;*
Crows in the Snow
Patricia Pfahl *(Canada) Poems: How To Love A Woman;*
The Hammock; Obsidian
Bonnie Roberts *(USA) Poems: Daddy, Who Cut The Moon In Half;*
Swimming Home To Myself
Sayed H. Rohani *(Afghanistan) Poem: Tales of Love*
Peter Alan Soron *(UK) Poem: Click here to make a million*
Cigeng Zhang *(China) Poem: What was left*

The Poetic Bond III (2013)

ISBN-10: 1492384194
ISBN-13: 978-1492384199

Christine Anderes (New York, USA) *Poems: Migration; The Moon Rides High In The Sky* / **Graham Bates** (Christchurch, New Zealand) *Poems: Rapture; Jazz Intelligence* / **Mark Beechill** (Kent, UK) *Poem: Back to Work* **Rebecca Behar** (Paris, France) *Poem: About Turner's Paintings of Venice I & II* **Nikki Bennett** (Merseyside, UK) *Poems: Hinge Cradled in its Own Cap; Thicker Skin* / **Rosalind Brenner** (New York, USA) *Poem: God's Rebuke* / **BJ Brown** (Connecticut, USA) *Poem: Edu-Can't Cry Sis* / **Ian Colville** (Bedfordshire, UK) *Poem: Waiting Bridge / The History of the Clothes Line in Medieval Europe* / **Clark Cook** (British Columbia, Canada) *Poem: Stopping Trains* / **William DiBenedetto** (Seattle, US) *Poems: Triton Beach; Angelo's Hat* / **Sam Doctors** (California, USA) *Poems: A Brindled Cast; A Supine Oak; In Praise of Stone Fences* / **Belinda Dupret** (West Sussex, UK) *Poem: The Scent of Honey* / **Sumita Dutta** (Chennai, India) *Poem: Her Flight* / **Nina Floreteng** (Haninge, Sweden) *Poem: The Shadow* / **Louise Francois** (Middlesex, UK) *Poem: Tomato 'Trumpet Red'* / **Gilbert A Franke** (Texas, USA) *Poem: Chief Joseph* / **GK Grieve** (London, UK) *Poem: The Anniversary* / **Seamus Harrington** (Cork, Eire) *Poem: The Hunters* / **Scott Hastie** (Hertfordshire, UK) *Poem: Life Collects* / **James Higgins** (Oregon, USA) *Poems: Family Trait; Party Manners* / **Robin Ouzman Hsilop** (South Yorkshire, UK) *Poems: Red Butteflies / From Here To Silence* / **Diane Jardel** (Eire) *Poem: Light and Shade* / **Mark L Levinson** (Israel) *Poems: The Book; The Agent* / **Carey Link** (Alabama, USA) *Poem: Where Am I?* / **Trevor Maynard** (Surrey, UK) *Poems: Beyond The Writing On The Wall; The Chattering Ants* / **Mermie** (UK) *Poems: Eggshells; The Eve Of Independence* / **Simon Miller** (Kent, UK) *Poem: Tingling Point* / **Linda Mills** (Oregon, USA) *Poems: A Cloud of Butterflies; Coal Taking* / **Marli Merker Moreira** (Brazil) *Poem: Vacant Eyes* / **Christine Pearson** (Maryland, USA) *Poem: I DIDN'T KNOW I LOVED* / **RH Peat** (California, USA) *Poem: Forgotten Embroidery* / **Bonnie Roberts** (Alabama, USA) *Spirit Animal; God's Opposable Thumb Leaves Me Feeling Uncomforted* / **Niek Satjin** (Amsterdam, Holland) *Poem: alles fängt an mit der Neugier* / **Sharla Lee Shults** (Georgia, USA) *Poem: Messages in the Wind* / **Peter Alan Soron** (UK) *Poem: Beard* **Charles Thielman** (Chicago, USA) *Poem: Faith in the Ruins* **Cigeng Zhang** (China) *Poem: Drunk Smile*

The Poetic Bond II (2012)

ISBN-10: 1480209732
ISBN-13: 978-1480209732

Christine Anderes (New York, USA) *Poem: The Power Of Circles* / **Frances Ayers** (New York, USA) *Poem: Grief Has No Hold* / **Graham Bates** (Christchurch, New Zealand) *Poem: Untitled* / **Rebecca Behar** (Paris, France) *Poem: The Tradition Man* / **JE Bird** (Surrey, UK) *Poem: Part of the Process* / **Lewis Bosworth** (Wisconsin, USA) *Poems: On Billy; Coloring Kids* / **Jessie Brown** (Massachusetts, USA) *Poems: Lucy Clifton Rising in the Northern Sky; Love Poem; Novenas* / **Robert Campion** (Surrey, UK) *Poem: Grey* / **Tim Coburn** (Cumbria, UK) *Poem: My Toybox was my treasure* / **Ian Colville** (Bedfordshire, UK) *Poem: Timed Out* / **James Darcy** (Hampshire, UK) *Poem: Alone* / **Sam Doctors** (California, USA) *Poem: A Time Suspended* / **Belinda Dupret** (West Sussex, UK) *Poem: Fruitful* / **Nina Floreteng** (Haninge, Sweden) *Poem: Spring of Awakening* / **Gilbert A Franke** (Texas, USA) *Poem: The Stocking Cap* / **William Gregory** (Kent, UK) *Poem: The Unseen* / **Robin Ouzman Hislop** (South Yorkshire, UK) *Poem: Far from Equilibrium* / **Rachel Z Ikins** (New York, USA) *Poem: Beneath a Saturn Sky* / **Romi Jain** (Jaipur, India) *Poem: Would you come to me?* / **Diane Jardel** (Eire) *Poem: Grass* / **Cathriona Lafferty** (Alava, Spain) *Poem: A Love in Chains* / **John Lambremont Snr** (Louisiana, USA) *Poem: To My Octogenarian* / **Frieda W Landau** (Florida, USA) *Poem: When the Revolution was Young* / **Naomi Madelin** (Bristol, UK) *Poem: When you meet me* / **Trevor Maynard** (Surrey, UK) *Poems: Gently, I walk the water's edge; My love is like the ocean* / **Marli Merker Moreira** (Brazil) *Poem: First Kiss* / **Miklos Mezosi** (Budapest, Hungary) *Poem: Farewell! Do spend thy time and money well!* / **Linda Mills** (Oregon, USA) *Poem: From My Eye* / **Robert Prattico** (Massachusetts, USA) *Poem: Poetry is Dead* / **Nancy Pritchard** (Missouri, USA) *Poems: Dreaming in an Alley; Allusions* / **Bonnie Roberts** (Alabama, USA) Poem: *In Lieu of Flowers* / **Nancy Scott** (New Jersey, USA) *Poem The Poor Man's Bride* / **Sharla Lee Shults** (Georgia, USA) *Poem: Echoes in Wartime* / **Peter Alan Soron** (not disclosed) *Poem: in quietness and green* / **Antony Taylor** (Texas, USA) *Poem: The Barber* / **Janet Gell Thompson** (Derbyshire, UK) *Poem: Little Lacemakers* / **Tom Watts** (Bristol, UK) *Poem: On Visiting El Castellon* / **Ann Widdicor** (Norway) *Poem: Spent Aquilegia* / **Michaelle Yarborough** (North Carolina, USA) *Poem: Tank*

The Poetic Bond (2011)

ISBN (10) 1466498412
ISBN (13) 978-1466498419

George Chijioke Amadi (Lagos, Nigeria) *Poem: A Wife's Neck Saved* / **Graham Bates** (Christchurch, New Zealand) *Poem: Touch* **Marguerite Guzman Bouvard** (Massachusetts, USA) *Poems: Bougainvillea; Invisible* / **Dan Brook** (California, USA) *Poem: November Ninth* / **Bonnie Gail Carter** (Indiana, USA) *Poems: I Will; The Chill Turned Warm* **Alexander Clarke** (Michigan, USA) *Poem: Status Update* **Durand J. Compton** (Kansas, USA) *Poem: IT IS A FINE IRISH MORNING* **Laurie Corzett** (undisclosed) *Poem: Under Cover of Lightning* **Marian Dunn** (Lancashire, England) *Poem: Watching the War* **A.D. Fallon** (Kentucky, USA) *Poem: Futility of Desire* **James Gilmore** (California, USA) *Poem: My 30th* **Sandra Hanks** (Seychelles, Indian Ocean) *Poem: "Moon Shine Supine"* / **Chi Holder** (Missouri, USA) *Poem: Enduring the Storm* **Romi Jain** (California, USA) *Poem: Her New Abode* **Diane Margaret Jardel** (Co.Fermanagh, Northern Ireland) Poem: The Mirror / **Michael Lee Johnson** (Illinois, USA) *Poems: Charley Plays a Tune; Kentucky Blue* / **Just Kribbe** (California, USA) *Poem: Telegram* **Drake Mabry** (Poitiers, France) *Poems: Four Haiku* **Trevor Maynard** (Surrey, England) *Poems: Redundant C; elegant grace eternal* / **Marli Merker Moreira** (Burgos, Spain) *Poem: Dead Woman* **Debbie Edwards Morton** (Ohio, USA) *Poem: What Will Happen?* **Gillian Prew** (Argyll, Scotland) *Poem: Birds and Bombs* / **Nancy Pritchard** (Missouri, USA) *Poems: Moon Madness; Trouble on the Line* **Sarah Rahman** (Karachi, Pakistan) *Poem: The Worrying Whys Within* / **Rainbow Reed** (England) *Poem: The Storm* / **Gill C Shaw** (Lancashire, England) *Poem: Peace of Big Bear* / **Michael Shepherd** (Somerset, England) *Poem: In Expectation of Rain* / **Peter Alan Soron** (undisclosed) *Poems: the grand I; Tough Call in E.Z. City* / **Tom Spencer** (Indiana, USA) *Poem: Festival of Souls* / **N. A'Yara Stein** (Indiana, USA) *Poems: Saudade; La Nuit Blanche* / **Ashleigh Stevens** (London, England) *Poem: I feel like dancing in the night* / **Tom Watts** (Surrey, England) *Poem: The World's Waif* **Mark Jason Welch** (Barbados, West Indies) *Poem: The Truth about Oranges*

Poetry by Trevor Maynard

Grey Sun, Dark Moon (2015)
ISBN-10: 1517095255
ISBN-13: 978-1517095253

Keep on Keepin' On (2012)
ISBN-10: 1480052493
ISBN-13: 978-1480052499

Love, Death, and the War on Terror (2009)
ISBN-10: 1445206625
ISBN-13: 978-1445206622

Plays by Trevor Maynard

Four Truths (2012)
Compilation of four one-act plays
ISBN-10: 1466453397
ISBN-13: 978-1466453395

Glass (2010)
ISBN-10: 1445233231
ISBN-13: 978-1445233239

From Pillow To Post (2010)
ISBN-10: 0955851416
ISBN-13: 978-0955851414

Willowdown Books Catalogue

Life Dances (2017)
Sandy Norris, Lynne Zotalis, Maria Borland, Michael McLaughlin, Belinda DuPret, and Israela Margalit
An anthology of six short stories edited by Trevor Maynard
ISBN: 978-1978098039

The Poetic Bond VII (2017)
International poetry anthology
ISBN: 978-1978098039

The Poetic Bond VI (2016)
International poetry anthology
ISBN: 978-1539334682

Echoes in the Earth (2016)
by Pushpita Awasthi
Collected poems edited by Trevor Maynard
ISBN: 978-1533618801

Grey Sun, Dark Moon (2015)
by Trevor Maynard
A collection of poems
ISBN: 978-1517095253

The Poetic Bond V (2015)
International poetry anthology
ISBN: 978-1517783808

The Poetic Bond IV (2014)
International poetry anthology
ISBN: 978-1503034525

The Poetic Bond III (2013)
International poetry anthology
ISBN: 978-1492384199

Keep on Keepin' On (2012)
by Trevor Maynard
A collection of poetry
ISBN: 978-1480052499

The Poetic Bond II (2012)
International poetry anthology
ISBN: 978-1480209732

The Poetic 8ond (2011)
International poetry anthology
ISBN: 978-1466498419

Four Truths (2011)
by Trevor Maynard
Four one act plays (1989-1996)
"She", "From Pillow to Post", "Graye", and "Taciturn"
ISBN, 978-1466453395

From Pillow to Post (2010)
by Trevor Maynard
One-act play (1991)
ISBN 978-0955851414

Glass (2010)
by Trevor Maynard
A full length play (1996)
ISBN 978-1445233239

The Watcher from the Beacon (2010)
by Peter Alan Soron
Poetry collection by Trevor Maynard
ISBN-13: 978-1480108806

Love, Death, and the War of Terror (2009)
by Trevor Maynard
ISBN 978-1445206622

Eulogy for my Grandfather,
George William Maynard 1916 -2001

My grandfather was a big man – tall in stature – full of heart –
Big White Father Christmas Beard – Big Voice –
a larger than life personality and a fantastic character.

There are a million and one stories to tell about him, and, telling a story, *with a few slightly colourful* additions to the truth, is something we've all learnt from him.

In the Second World War, he was a paratrooper, which basically meant that aeroplanes would fly him to places and throw him out from several thousand feet, sometimes into the desert, sometimes into Italy, and once into a pineapple field. One story goes that, lost in North Africa, Granpop's CO ordered him; "Maynard, go over that sand dune and find some food and water." Six hours later he returned, miraculously carrying oranges and water. What his CO didn't know, of course, was that there was quite literally an oasis just over the sand dune. Back in Europe, he found himself dropped amongst a load of surrendering Italians with a lot of spare equipment. It was obvious what he had to do; barter the tyres off the Italians and sell them to the incoming *Yanks*.

Recently he perfected the art of staying on an aeroplane until it landed, flying off to America every year, sometimes twice a year. Granpop had become quite the jetsetter. One year he returned with a specially painted walking stick that had special powers; he knew this was true because it was given to him by a witchdoctor on an Indian Reservation, apparently. When not flying in an aeroplane Granpop was often to be found flying down to the bingo in his chariot; though, of course he could have gone a lot faster if he had convinced his sons, Brin and Ken, to fit the supercharged engine he was after. With the new engine the chariot would have achieved a cruising speed of twelve miles an hour!

Another enduring vision is that of the Maynard's Sweet Stall in the market – (not that other lot of wine-gum making bunch of fakes) – but us, the REAL Maynard's – with the apostrophe!
Granpop travelled all over with his candy making machine – to Wales, to Cornwall, to Scotland, to the Nottingham Goose Fayre: and the patter and the spiel became ever more colourful with every

trip "I have sold these sweets to the King and Queen," he'd say, adding; "And the Jack, the Ace, the ten, nine, eight, seven, six, five, four, three and two."

Often he took his kids with him, and usually he would return with them; but occasionally he would leave them on a hill in Wales and tell them to make their own way back.

Granpop spent years on the cabs in Southend, one of the originals with AC, and later he ran a café in the Market. When you'd go in, he would ask you if you wanted your toast well done, and if you said yes, when it popped up out of the toaster – he'd clap his hands and tell the bread "Well-Done".

All the old boys and old girls would come into the café and call him Young George, even though for the most part they were younger than him. He'd give them a cup of tea, then send them on their way with a cheery smile – "Another Cadburys!" He'd say.
He was always a bit of a magnet for the Cadbury's Fruit and Nutcase. Even last year when he visited the hospital, Granpop woke up at three in the morning to find some old boy had nicked his cap and slippers and was sitting stark-naked in the chair next to Granpop's bed. "See that one, boy," He told his sons, next day. "Another Cadburys."

We all play cards in the Maynard family, and we all win; *or at least we would win if the other players could actually play the game properly.* But the game I'll remember Granpop for is quoits, or horseshoes. Granpop was an expert at knocking a leaning horseshoe onto the peg. Granpop also spent many a Saturday as a marshal at Roots Hall, a dedicated Blues Supporter throughout his life. His sense of fun and playing games is something we have all inherited from him; along with our wonderful singing voices; heard to best effect in performing "Alloetta". The part about "how I love your curly teeth" always particularly reminded me of Granpop. "Toothache, boy?" He'd say. "I haven't had any trouble with me teeth for sixty years; had 'em all whipped out when I was twenty-three!"

A few years on – and pushing eighty, Granpop worked down the seafront in the arcades, still having a laugh with the punters as they gave him a pound and he gave them ninety pence in change – the other ten pence slipping gracefully into his pocket –

And then one year there were these mini-carriage clocks –
I don't know where he got them from, but we all got one for Christmas that year.

Talking of Christmas – Granpop was the real father Christmas, and for the last twenty years, he has been donning the red uniform and trimming his *real* white beard, then sitting in the big chair in his Santa's Grotto in Keddies; or sometimes he'd drop in on children's parties with a big sack of presents. Every time a child doubted the existence of Santa Claus, Granpop would tell them to tug his beard, and when they did, their eyes would light up, because then they knew, Father Christmas is *REAL.*

One of Granpop's proudest moments I remember, was when he and Nan celebrated their fiftieth wedding anniversary – all the kids, grandkids, great grandkids, brothers, sisters, cousins, friends, Uncle Tom Cobbley and all, were in attendance, and he and Nan were King and Queen of the Maynards. I remember the photograph of them that always sat in the centre of their mantelpiece; it appeared in the local paper. Over fifty years they were married.

Eighty-five years he lived - *thirty past the time the bingo caller first tried to call his number;* but Granpop wasn't having any of that.

Now though, *is his time to relent.*

He saw many new great grandchildren born at the end of the twentieth century and he saw in the New Millennium and beyond.

Now is his time to join his Renee and to join their baby son,
both of whom he loved all his life and missed so terribly.

And we, his children, grandchildren, great-grandchildren, family and friends, will miss him terribly, but will always remember him with fond memories.

(Read by Trevor Maynard at the funeral of his grandfather, George Maynard, 2002)

Love, light, and peace

Made in the USA
Monee, IL
18 November 2019